Harry the Poisonous Centipede goes to Sea

The third
adventure about

Harry the Poisonous Centipede

ALSO BY LYNNE REID BANKS

Harry the Poisonous Centipede
Harry the Poisonous Centipede's
Big Adventure

The Indian in the Cupboard
Return of the Indian
The Mystery of the Cupboard
The Secret of the Indian
The Key to the Indian

Broken Bridge
The Dungeon
One More River

Harry the Poisonous Centipede goes to Sea

Lynne Reid Banks

Illustrated by Tony Ross

HarperCollins *Children's Books*

For Paloma and David

Harry the Poisonous Centipede Goes to Sea
Text copyright © 2006 by Lynne Reid Banks
Illustrations copyright © 2006 by Tony Ross
All rights reserved. Printed in the United States of America.
No part of this book may be used or reproduced in any manner whatsoever without written
permission except in the case of brief quotations embodied in critical articles and reviews.
For information address HarperCollins Children's Books, a division of HarperCollins
Publishers, 1350 Avenue of the Americas, New York, NY 10019.
www.harperchildrens.com

Library of Congress Cataloging-in-Publication Data
Banks, Lynne Reid, date
   Harry the poisonous centipede goes to sea / Lynne Reid Banks ; illustrated by Tony Ross.
—1st ed.
      p.   cm.
   Summary: The further adventures of Harry and George, two young poisonous centipedes,
as they travel across the sea to a mysterious new land filled with dangerous Hoo-Mins.
   ISBN-10: 0-06-077548-3 (trade bdg.) — ISBN-13: 978-0-06-077548-3 (trade bdg.)
   ISBN-10: 0-06-077549-1 (lib. bdg.) — ISBN-13: 978-0-06-077549-0 (lib. bdg.)
   1. Centipedes—Juvenile fiction.   [1. Centipedes—Fiction.   2. Insects—Fiction.]
I. Ross, Tony, ill.   II. Title.
PZ10.3.B2155Has 2006   2005028766
[Fic]—dc22   CIP
                                                                        AC

1 2 3 4 5 6 7 8 9 10
❖
First Edition

1. How It Began

Harry and George were lying in the moonlight. They'd gone up to the no-top-world as soon as it got dark—looking for an adventure, George had said, but there didn't seem to be one. Harry had his suspicions that George wasn't so much looking for adventure as for Something Else.

These aren't people we're talking about. They're centipedes. And not those little wiggly wire-worms you dig up in your garden, either. These are giant tropical centipedes, and they are *poisonous*. They have pincers on their heads to defend themselves with, and also—I have to be perfectly frank—to kill things with, by biting them and paralyzing them with their poison.

Terrible, you think? Cruel? Oh, please. This is the Natural World. Not many creatures in nature get by without eating some other creature, and that includes most Hoo-Mins.

What's a Hoo-Min? Well, you're going to have to do a bit of guessing in this story anyhow, so you can start with Hoo-Mins. If you reckon giant poisonous centipedes are scary, it may surprise you to know they're much more scared of us. *Us Hoo-Mins.* Get it? Right. We're the Hoo-Mins. That's your first puzzle solved.

Hoo-Mins, or rather H-Mns, is Centiped-ish, the language of centipedes. They mainly use signals, but they can crackle very faintly to one another, and when they do there are no vowel sounds. So you must realize at once that their real names couldn't be Harry and George. That's just what I call them. Their real, Centipedish names were Hxzltl and Grnddjl.

Go on. Try to say them. Try to say your *own* name without the a's, e's, i's, o's, and u's (I'll let you keep the y's) and you'll be talking Centipedish.

I must just add that of course centipedes don't have words for a lot of things that they don't know much about, so they've become very good at inventing ways to describe them. You'll find a lot of these centi-descriptions in this story. I'm sure you'll be able to work them out, but I'll just give you a couple of examples. (Don't worry—the story's going to start at any minute!)

Hoo-Mins are the enemies
of centipedes. But they
have others. There are
also hairy-biters
(which is anything
hairy that bites),

flying-swoopers (birds, of
course, plus maybe bats),
and belly-crawlers. No
prizes for guessing that
one—it's snakes.

But Hoo-Mins are in a category all by
themselves. The category of the fastest,
biggest, and scariest things around.

Harry and George lived underground in
earth-tunnels, which are nice and damp

(it's very important to centipedes not to Dry Out), and came up at night to hunt. You'll soon find out that their favorite foods were *not* things that you'd fancy.

When they were younger, they were centis, which are child centipedes. But now they were cent*eens,* about seven inches long—nearly as big as Belinda. Belinda was Harry's mother and George's adopted mother. *Her* Centipedish name—are you ready for this? —was Bkvlbbchk.

Belinda was getting quite old now, though she could still give a toad or a beetle a run for its money—it was just the very fast things like lizards and mice she had trouble with. So Harry and George did some of her hunting for her. They'd had lots of cuticle-rippling adventures and feeler-close escapes, but they always managed to get back home in the end. So she'd decided to stop poison-claw-clicking, which is how mother centipedes nag, and let them have their freedom.

"Just take care," she would beg, as they headed out of their home tunnels up into the dark-time.

"We'll be all right, Mama," Harry would say as he chased after George, who still usually led the way. "We'll bring you back something delicious for end-of-dark-time meal!"

So, on this night (night—dark-time—okay?), they'd done some hunting and had a tasty heap of goodies beside them. These included a couple of slugs, three assorted caterpillars, one large rhinoceros beetle— which had put up quite a fight but they'd overpowered it in the end—and a mouse. This was their big prize because they knew Belinda loved a tasty bit of mouse before she went to sleep for the bright-time. All right, I'll help you out this time—the day.

"Mama will be really pleased with us," Harry said contentedly as they lay there resting, feeling the pale, un-hot light of white ball shining down on them. It wasn't a full ball tonight or they would have scuttled underground to escape it—they didn't like too much light, being night creatures.

"Apart from the beetle, though," mused George, "we can't say any of it was very exciting." He didn't seem to be enjoying the rest. Half his twenty-one segments were off the ground and he was waving his feelers around in all directions.

"Why don't you relax, Grndd?" asked Harry rather peevishly. "We've got enough food. Do you want a snack?"

"No," said George.

"So what are you questing around for?"

George didn't answer. He dropped to

his forty-two feet and took off without another crackle.

Harry was feeling rather lazy after his night's hunting and for once he didn't follow. He pretty well guessed what George had gone after. It wasn't food. He'd sensed the Something Else. The Something Else was a centeena.

Yes, George was into girls. Girl-centipedes, that is. Only Harry didn't feel quite ready for all that yet. So he gave a centipedish sigh, laid his head on the good, warm earth, and waited.

Harry loved the no-top-world. It was so full of interesting smells and sounds. Of course he knew it could be dangerous. Apart from Hoo-Mins, which didn't usually hunt at night, there were all those flying-swoopers and hairy-biters and belly-crawlers that I told you about to watch out for.

But then there was danger everywhere. When he was a young centi, Hoo-Mins had pushed a cloud of white-choke down into the centipedes' tunnels and nearly killed all the little creatures that lived in them. There was always the fear that water would flood down and drown them when the Big Dropping Damp came, or that a thinner-than-usual belly-crawler would creep down in the bright-time and grab them as they lay asleep under their leaves.

There were hairy-biters that could dig, too. Belinda told stories about another nest she'd lived in, which had been dug up by a big ugly hairy-biter. It simply wrecked the whole beautiful maze of tunnels that the centipedes and other tunnel-dwellers had carefully burrowed, and ate everything that hadn't run away fast enough.

Yes, it was a dangerous world, even for a big, strong, poisonous centeen like Harry.

Still, it was a good world, too, when nothing was going wrong. And nothing was going wrong tonight. It couldn't have been more peaceful.

Harry waited for George until he got fed up, and then he decided to start shifting their prey down the tunnels to where Belinda was waiting. George could bring more when he got back.

Harry was just trying to decide whether he could get the mouse down the hole whole, or if he should do it a leg at a time, when he sensed George's signal.

"Hx! Come quick, I've found something!"

2. George's Big Find

When Harry heard George's signal he forgot all about being tired. He raced off, leaving the pile of prey unguarded. It probably wouldn't have been there when they got back.

Only, they didn't get back.

He found George standing on his rear legs examining the sides of a straight-up-hard-thing. It was something Harry didn't like the look of—some kind of trap.

"Grndd! Come away from that—it looks like a can't-get-out!" crackled

Harry, always the cautious one.

"No, it's not! Look, there are long openings. You can easily get in *and* out of it. And look what's inside!"

Harry stood tall beside George and stuck his head in through one of the long holes. The straight-up-hard-thing was full of tree-droppings.

Harry, like nearly all centipedes, was a meat-eater. He'd never eaten the stuff that fell down from trees. So all those yellow-curves didn't interest him. But there was some kind of meat in there too. He could smell it. Spiders, he thought.

Harry dropped onto all forty-twos again.

"We've got enough, Grndd," he said reasonably. "I don't feel like hunting any-more."

George gave him a look of scorn.

"Oh, come on, Hx! It's those big furry juicy ones. Just *one*! They're my favorites!"

Harry was remembering that Belinda loved tarantula, especially the heads. She was really too old to catch them for herself anymore.

"Oh—all right then," said Harry. And he followed George through one of the long holes, which, in case you haven't guessed, were actually gaps in a crate of bananas.

They followed the tarantula smell—unmistakable—into the bottom of the crate. The great spider was asleep, but it woke up with a jump as it felt them coming. It scurried on its hairy legs under a curved bunch of bananas, but George raced round to the other side of the banana-tunnel. They homed in on it from each side and stopped it before it was even properly awake. "Stopped" means "killed" in Centipedish—they don't like saying "killed" because it sounds too nasty.

"I must say, it smells wonderful," said Harry. "What do you think, could we just have a nibble?" He was feeling suddenly starving after all their exertions.

"We'll have to," said practical George. "It's too big to squeeze it out through those long holes unless we chew a bit off its big fat abdomen."

"Don't touch the head, though. We must save that for Mama."

Well, before long the head was all that was left. And George was looking pretty hungrily at that, but Harry drew the  line and said, with a centi-burp, "We've had enough, Grndd. Come on, we must go home now or big-yellow-ball will be coming back and then we might Dry Out."

I ought to stress that, short of something *getting* them, Drying Out is the worst thing that can happen to centipedes. The rims of the breathing-holes along their backs have to stay damp or they can't breathe, so they're naturally very careful. In fact, if you're a centipede, saying you're "Dried-Out" is like saying you're done for.

They went up through the layers of bananas to the first long hole and tried to climb through it. But they were so full of tarantula that they found it was going to be a very tight squeeze indeed. Especially for Harry, who held the tarantula's head in his poison-claw.

"We shouldn't have eaten so much," said Harry.

"I just couldn't seem to stop," said George. "Hm. Well. I suppose we'd better just curl up and have a nap till our meal has gone through and we're thin again."

So that's what they did. They found a comfortable place among the bananas and fell asleep, curled up together with the head in between them, so no one could take it away.

If they'd only known it, that was the least of their worries.

3. The No-meat-feeder

They did a bit more than take a nap.

Many poisonous creatures can eat each other and not get poisoned themselves, but perhaps in this case some of the tarantula's poison got into them, just enough to make them really sleepy. Because otherwise it's hard to explain how they didn't wake up when day came and the crate of bananas they were in was picked up by a forklift, loaded onto a big transporter, and carried far from the banana plantation it had been in—far from their home-tunnel, far from Belinda. By the time they woke up, if they'd run their fastest for a week of nights, they couldn't have found their way home.

Well. George had wanted an adventure. But this was going to be a lot more than even he had bargained for.

"Grndd!"

Harry woke up first. The straight-up-hard-thing was moving. It was jiggling. The curved "hands" of bananas were jiggling too, and all the small creatures hiding among them, including Harry and George, were being shaken around.

Some had been dislodged from their

hiding or sleeping places amid the fruit and had fallen to the bottom of the crate, where the centeens could hear them scuttling about anxiously. Harry, especially, was good at understanding other species' signals. Now he thought, "There's a lot of fear in here!"

"What's happening?" asked George in alarm.

"I don't know. We're moving."

With one accord, the two centeens scurried to the nearest long hole, the one they'd tried to squeeze out of before they fell asleep. They put their heads out. Their weak little eye clusters could just make out bright light (which they hated) and lots of colors and patterns moving past them.

"Where are we? We're not where we were last night!" crackled George.

"I told you! This is a can't-get-out! I said

we shouldn't come in here!"

"It's not a can't-get-out, Hx. We can get out any time we like."

"So what's stopping us?"

They stood side by side on a banana, trying to get their bearings. They were far from the ground—that was obvious. They could see it racing past underneath them. "It's a long way down," said George.

"If we leave here, we'll Dry Out," said Harry. Big-yellow-ball was shining hotly. They could feel the heat in the air and see the brightness outside the crate. The heat where they lived was a very damp kind of heat. They sensed they'd be all right as long as they stayed in the moist darkness inside the crate.

"We'd better wait till the moving stops," said Harry. "And see what it's like then."

Meanwhile they tried to behave as if everything was all right, even though they both knew it wasn't. They went back to their curved nest of bananas. Harry noticed something at once.

"Where's Mama's head?"

"Her what?" asked George blankly.

"The tarantula head we saved for her! It's gone," said Harry.

"Maybe it just rolled away somewhere."

"No. I wedged it in tightly between these yellow-curves," Harry said. "Someone must have stolen it!"

They began to quest around them. George suddenly froze.

"Hx, there's one of us somewhere in here!"

Harry got it too, now. A decidedly pleasant aroma, amid all the whiffs of other, alien creatures like flies, beetles, and spiders. Another centipede, certainly, but—different. Different from him, different from George.

"It's my centeena!" crackled George softly.

"*Your* centeena?"

"Well . . . er . . . no, not exactly. I mean . . . I was chasing her—last night—I hadn't really caught up with her. I was looking for her, you know, following her scent, when I found the straight-up-hard-thing with the tarantula inside."

"She must've got in before us. She's here with us."

"Right!" said George eagerly. "Let's find her!"

It wasn't hard. Although the crate was big and there were lots of bananas filling most of it, there were plenty of little spaces and chinks where small creatures could hide. As the two centeens searched, they realized that, whatever else might happen, they weren't going to be short of a bite to eat.

They sent out inviting signals, and after a while a little female head poked out from between two big bunches of bananas.

"Hello," she signaled shyly. "Did you call?" Of course they hadn't *called*. Centipedes can't *call*. That's just my way of putting it.

Harry watched her creep out until she was in full smell. George immediately went up to her and touched feelers with her, and ran all around her once in greeting.

"I'm Grndd and this is Hx," he said. "What's your name?"

"I'm Jgnblm," she said. All right, no, I'm not proposing to go on trying to write that or expecting you to say it, though I should add that both the centeens thought Jgnblm was a most euphonious name, which means that to them it had a sweet sound.

Let's see, then. What about Josie?

"What are you doing here?" Harry asked, touching feelers with her very shyly. He'd never touched feelers with a centeena before, except Belinda, of course. It felt very nice.

"He was chasing me," she said, meaning George. "So I just ducked in through one of those long holes to hide."

"Why didn't you get out again before it started to move?"

"I don't know. I think I just liked it in here. I like yellow-curves," she added, indicating the banana she was standing on.

"You like standing on them?" asked Harry.

"Eating them," she said.

"You *eat* tree-droppings?" asked George incredulously.

"Yes."

"I notice you like tarantula heads, too," remarked Harry bitterly.

Josie looked puzzled. "What do you mean, tarantula heads?"

"Well, didn't you just take one from here?"

"No," she said. "I don't like eating things that have been alive; it makes me feel a bit sick, so I eat lots of different tree-droppings."

"Wait a minute. You don't mean you *never* eat ordinary things?"

"No. Just tree-droppings," she said demurely.

There was a silence.

"Hx, she's a no-meat-feeder," crackled George under his breath.

27

A centipede that didn't like meat and wouldn't *stop* anything! They waved their feelers at Josie as if she were not completely centipede.

"Please don't feeler me like that," she said. "It's rather rude."

"Oh! Sorry," said George at once. "It's just—I've never met a no-meat-feeder before. What kind of—er—tree-droppings do you like best? I've never really bothered to try any."

"There are so many different kinds!" Josie said eagerly. "One never gets to the end of them!"

"Weird," crackled George. Harry nudged him with a bump of his middle section.

"I don't think it's weird," said Harry. "It's interesting. At least you won't be hungry in here with all these yellow-curves. I wish I liked them."

"Try one," said Josie.

To oblige her, Harry bent his head and took a bite.

"Ugh!" he said. "It's horrible!"

Josie gave a centipedish laugh by shaking all her segments up and down. "No, no, not the outside! You have to get through to the soft, sweet stuff inside." She caught a ridge of the yellow skin between her poison-claws and neatly stripped it back. "Now try again," she said.

George backed away. But Harry nibbled a little of the soft white stuff, and then a little more. "Hm. It's not bad, I must say. Soft as worms. But not a bit like them to taste."

Josie shuddered daintily. "I couldn't bear to eat a worm!" she said.

Before any more could be crackled, the jiggling movement stopped. The three of them dashed along a bridge of bananas to

the long opening again and stuck their
heads out.

"Smell that, Grndd! You know what that
is, don't you?" Harry said in shocked tones.

"Yeah, I'm afraid I do," said George.
"It's the no-end puddle."

"The no-end puddle? What's that?" asked Josie.

"It's water," said Harry. "Water and water and water, more than you'd ever think there could be. It goes on and on forever—that's why it's called no-end. It's not even water you can drink, either."

"Can you swim?" George asked Josie abruptly.

"Swim? You mean, like marine centipedes do?"

"Except they don't," said George. "But I can, and so can Harry, and if by any horrible chance we're going to get dropped in the no-end puddle, like we once were, you're going to have to learn to swim very fast indeed."

Poor Josie crouched down on her banana and put out signals of fear. "I can't, I know I can't!" she waickled (you know—a wailing crackle.) "If I'm dropped in the no-end puddle, I'll *stop!*"

Both the centeens rushed to her side.

"No, you won't," they both said. "You won't, because we're here, and we'll look after you!" And then they looked at each other across her cuticle, and their feelers stuck up straight, which meant, "Why are *you* crackling that to her? *I'm* crackling that to her!"

Oh, dear. Centeenas. They can cause trouble even when they don't mean to. It's not their fault, of course.

And just in case you were wondering what did happen to the head, since Josie hadn't eaten it . . . Well, I'm sorry to tell you that *another tarantula* had sneaked up through the bananas and grabbed it. Not very nice, tarantulas.

In fact, the word "cannibal" comes to mind.

4. Centeens at Sea

Quite a long time passed. The three centeens crouched together amid the yellow-curves and tried to keep their centi-spirits up by sending one another hopeful signals. Then the straight-up-hard-thing began to move again.

This time it moved sharply upward and then sideways. What was happening was that they were being swung through the air on the end of a crane, to be loaded aboard a ship. But they didn't know that. When they poked their heads out of the long hole and looked down, they couldn't make out *anything* underneath them. They were too high up.

All they knew was that there was a big bump, which made everything in the crate jump, and then there was no more bright light. That was a relief to them. There were a lot of vibrations and loud noises and after a while it got really dark (that was when the hatches went up on deck.) The centeens looked and feelered about them.

"Well, here we are—wherever we are," said George, quite cheerfully. "At least we're not going to drown."

"But what *is* going to happen?" asked Josie fearfully.

"Who knows?" said George. "It's a real adventure, anyway!"

Harry didn't say anything. He was thinking it was too much of an adventure for his taste, and that Belinda would be worried sick. She was old and it wasn't right to leave her like this. He looked at Josie, who was huddled up small at his side. "Do *you* want an adventure?" he asked her.

"I want my basket," she crackled faintly. Not many centeens even remember that their mothers once kept them in special little containers like baskets when they first came out of their eggs, but "I want my basket" is still what they say when they're feeling miserable and homesick and scared.

Harry was just going to crackle something comforting when George came over and boldly twisted his feelers around Josie's.

"Don't you worry, Jgn. I'm right beside you. I won't let anything bad happen."

She rubbed her head against his gratefully. "Thank you, Grndd," she said.

Harry lifted one feeler quizzically, and George saw it and looked away. He knew it meant, "Promises, promises." George couldn't really stop anything bad from happening and George knew Harry knew that, but Josie didn't know, and Harry wasn't mean enough to tell her.

At last a different movement began. It was a sort of slow rocking and swaying, and it went on and on. Sometimes it was a very strong, frightening movement that threw them about and had them slipping and sliding among the bananas. Sometimes it was quite gentle. They got used to it, and began to think of their nest in the yellow-curves as a sort of home away from home.

The worst thing by far was the cold. They weren't used to being cold and they had no defense against it. Luckily for them, this wasn't a refrigeration ship—you can't freeze bananas—but the hold was kept chilled to keep the fruit fresh on its journey, and this was very hard on the centeens. They had to keep moving about as much as possible. As for keeping damp, this was a major problem too.

What they did in the end was venture out of the crate and explore the hold of the ship until they came to a crate that held potatoes.

Potatoes are generally stored and shipped with earth around them. Earth is damp, and this was how the centeens managed not to Dry Out. But there weren't many living creatures in the dirt, so they had to keep returning to their original straight-up-hard-thing to find food.

There was no shortage for any of them. Quite a lot of creatures had found their way into the crate along with the bananas, including the second tarantula. Before the voyage ended, most of them had ended, too.

Josie happily ate banana. She wouldn't be tempted by any of the spiders, beetles, or even a small and very tasty snake that the others brought her.

"No, really. I couldn't," she would say, humping her midsections in polite disgust and turning her head away. "I'll just eat my nice yellow-curve, thank you."

"Aren't you getting bored with it?" asked Harry after three nights and days.

"Yes, but it doesn't matter," she said. "No-meat-feeders like us must not make a fuss." This is a direct quote from Beetle, a language that always rhymes. If any Hoo-Min vegetarians among you would like to use it—please, be my guest.

"All the more for us then," said George, who was a bit hurt that she didn't like anything he brought her.

But despite Josie's no-meat-feeder-ism, they liked her. And she liked them. As time passed, they crackled a lot to one another. Harry and George told Josie about their adventures, and she told them about some that she'd had. They already knew from Belinda that centias could be brave. But when Josie told them about a time when she'd gone up a tree to escape from a hairy-biter, been swooped at by a flying-swooper, fallen off right onto a Hoo-Min's head, and then run down his whole huge body ("Almost as big as the tree!") with him whacking at her with his big front feet and got away, they thought she was almost as brave as they were.

After many days and nights, the ship docked and the crates in the hold started to be unloaded.

The centeens realized that a change was happening. There was light again, coming from above. Soon their straight-up-hard-thing was swinging upward and then downward.

It wasn't
long before
they were moving
again, the same jiggling
noisy movement they'd felt
before. There was no doubt
now that they were a long, long
way from home, because the smells
were all different. And the air was, too.

"It's cooler here," Harry said,
questing about with his feelers.

"Drier, too," George said uneasily.

"Oh, I want my basket!"
moaned Josie.

"I thought no-meat-feeders
didn't fuss," said Harry.

"Only about food," Josie said.
"We can fuss about anything else."

"Speaking of food, we've
eaten everything," said Harry.

"I know," said George. "We'll have to

get out of here and hunt soon."

But it seemed to them a long time before the jiggling stopped and the crate was finally lowered to the ground.

There was a lot of noise going on all around them, and many new and alarming smells and vibrations. Most of it, they knew at once, came from Hoo-Mins. Peering out and feelering around, they could see and sense and smell them. The most gigantic, fast-moving, terrifying things in the world—and they were everywhere! Running around on their two legs, making loud noises to one another, and moving lots of big things from place to place.

"Hoo-Mins are so weird!" said George. "What are they all *doing*? They don't seem to be hunting, or eating, or tunneling—and what else is there? I can't make it out at all."

"Oh, I know!" said Josie. "It's do-

diddle. They do-diddle all the time; I've watched them."

"What's do-diddle?"

"It means rushing about doing things that don't make sense—that we'd never bother about. I don't know if it's to do with their food or their nests or what. It's just—*do-diddle.*"

They looked at her, puzzled and curious.

"Do you watch Hoo-Mins a lot, then?"

Josie looked rather uncomfortable. "Well, er—yes. I do watch them. From time to time. But I don't understand any of it really."

"Tell us more," said Harry.

"Well," Josie said. "This straight-up-hard-thing, for instance. I watched them do-diddle that. It wasn't like this to begin with. It was just flat pieces of a tree. After they'd do-diddled it, it was like it is now, a different shape, big enough to hold all these yellow-curves and move them about."

George and Harry looked at each other. She wasn't just a pretty poison-claw. She was clever.

"So what are they do-diddling now?" asked George.

They watched crackle-lessly for a while. Then Josie shrugged (a centipedish shrug, of course, by hunching her front two segments).

"They're just moving things about," she said. "They do that a lot. They've probably got some kind of plan, but I don't know what."

None of them did, but you can, because I'll tell you.

Their crate had been brought to a big covered market. All the bustling and do-diddling was the Hoo-Mins preparing to sell the produce inside them.

Pretty soon, there were screeching

noises and lots of vibrations and then light flooded down to the centeens through the chinks in the yellow-curves. Then, very quickly, the yellow-curves began to be taken away.

Instinctively the three centeens (please take this to mean two, and one centeena) fled down, through, and around the bunches of bananas to the very bottom of the crate. More and more bunches were lifted off, and soon there was only one more layer above to hide them from the Hoo-Mins.

"Let's get out of here!" said George.

They found a long hole near to the ground, and with George in the lead they squirmed through it.

A terrible uproar broke out among the Hoo-Mins.

"Blimey! Look at them horrible things!"

"Kill 'em!"

A big shadow fell on them. Harry knew what that meant! Something was trying to squash them!

"Run! Run your fastest!" he signaled wildly.

5. A Feeler-close Escape

Belinda had once told Harry a breathing-hole-stopping story about how she'd been chased by a Hoo-Min who was trying to stamp on her. She'd only just escaped.

Now Harry, George, and Josie found out what it's like to be chased by a whole crowd of Hoo-Mins, all trying to stamp on them.

It was absolutely terrifying. Big boots kept crashing down. Things were thrown at them. The only good thing was that there were three of them, all running madly in every direction, and this confused the Hoo-Mins who were trying to get them.

Two of them, bent on squashing Josie, banged straight into each other, bounced off, and fell over backward, nearly squashing George, who was behind

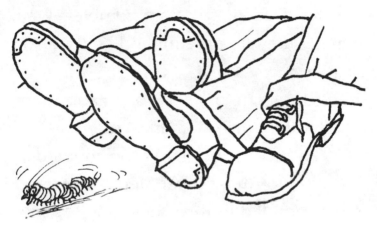

one of them. Another, his eyes fixed on the ground where Harry was ducking and weaving, lifted his heavy boot and tripped another Hoo-Min who was aiming for the same squirming, zig-zagging target.

In about ten seconds of our time—it seemed like forever to the centeens—the Hoo-Mins were in such a tangle they completely lost sight of the centeens. Each one had raced off in three different directions and dived under three different objects. They lay there, alone, trembling as only a centipede can tremble—well, actually they tremble much like us, a sort of quiver.

The foreman of the work gang came over to the tangle of market men.

"What's going on here?" he shouted.

The Hoo-Mins untangled themselves and scrambled to their feet.

"Sorry, guv. We was after some tropical centipedes that popped out of that crate. *Huge* great things they was, wasn't they, Kev?"

"I never seen anything like 'em. They must've been half as long as my arm!"

"Poisonous, them sort. Mate of mine got bitten by one once. Hand was paralyzed for a week."

The foreman scanned the floor for signs of squashed centipede.

"Well? So where are they?"

"Dunno, guv. They've gone."

"You mean, you let them escape?" roared the foreman.

"We couldn't help it! You should've seen 'em run! If they was horses, any one of 'em could've won the Derby!"

"Do you mean to tell me," yelled the foreman between clenched teeth, "that there are poisonous centipedes loose in this market just waiting to bite someone?"

There was a silence.

"Well, you'd better bloomin' well *find* 'em!" he shouted, and went stamping off.

There followed a halfhearted attempt to locate the fugitives, but it was soon given up, because the foreman started bellowing at them to *"get back to work!"*

After that, things quieted down a bit and the centeens emerged from their hiding places and started creeping around, keeping close to straight-up-hard-things, looking for one another.

Harry found Josie first. She came rushing up to him, in a state.

"Oh, Hx!" she crackled. "I'm so glad you're all right! I was so scared! I thought for sure we'd be stopped!"

Harry was only grateful she didn't mention anything about how the centeens had promised her they'd look after her and not let anything bad happen.

"Let's find Grndd," he said.

They soon did. But they got a shock.

"Grndd, you're hurt!" Josie crackled.

George had been hit a glancing blow by a bunch of bananas that had been hurled at him. Two of his back segments weren't working. He was dragging them along. The other two could see he was hurting badly and he couldn't move very fast at all.

He kept saying things like "It's not so bad, I'm all right," but they could see he wasn't. They hustled him under some big thing and got into the middle of it where it was dark and there was a nice damp place on the ground. The ground, of course, was not proper ground. It was something hard and cold and unyielding. You couldn't possibly dig in it. Harry had already noticed this. Not to be able to dig was a very serious matter.

"We're in a Place of Hoo-Mins," he said solemnly. "And we've got to get out of it to where we can find a tunnel. Or make one."

They lay under the big thing all day. They managed to get a bit of sleep; at least Harry and Josie did. George hurt too much. Centipedes aren't like dogs or cats, which can lick their hurts to help them heal. They just have to stay as still as possible and hope their bodies will get better by themselves. Luckily all bodies try their best to get better, and by the time night came, George was feeling—well, not as bad as before. He could move his injured segments a bit. But he didn't feel like doing any running, that was for sure.

At night the market went quiet for a few hours—all the Hoo-Mins went home and the lights were turned out and the big doors were locked. The centeens crept out at last and Harry and Josie quested around while George stayed still.

"We should go that way," reported Harry, pointing with his feelers. "I can smell earth, and there's a long hole we can get through." He meant the crack under one of the doors.

"Can you manage, Grndd?" asked Josie anxiously. "We can help you."

Which is what they did. Harry and Josie went on either side of George and they kind of nudged him along. But it was very slow.

"Perhaps you should leave me," George crackled after a while.

"Are you *crazy*?" said Harry. "We'll make it. Just keep your good legs moving."

6. Snacks in a Cold-hard

At last they crawled through the long hole and felt themselves in the no-top-world, which meant in the open. They sensed there was some earth nearby and that instantly made them feel much, much more centipede.

Harry went off exploring for a short time, and then came back. "I've found a lot of lovely soft earth," said Harry. "Let's dig a bright-time nest."

He didn't dare mention eating. He knew the others must be as hungry as he was.

He couldn't smell anything familiar in the way of food. Perhaps they didn't have any proper food in this strange place.

They were soon crawling up onto a loose pile of soil. To Harry's relief, the minute he and Josie started to dig, a number of tiny ants came rushing out. They were all much smaller than the ones the centeens were used to, but—
"So what! Grab them!" said George. Harry had his work cut out. The ants were quick and it was hard to catch hold of them, they were so tiny.

He barely managed to stop enough to give him and George a snack. George, who was obviously feeling better, complained bitterly that a centipede would need a whole nest of these ants to fill him up.

Josie sat there primly and wouldn't touch a thing.

Harry felt really uncomfortable, snapping up ants while Josie just sat there with her head turned away.

"Do you eat ants' *eggs*? They're not exactly meat," said Harry.

"Oh, yes, of course, I eat all kinds of eggs," she said.

So they dug some more and found part of the ants' nest. It had been disturbed and most of the eggs had been carried away, but there were enough to take at least the edge off Josie's appetite.

Actually, she did better than the others, because the eggs were bigger than the ants and you didn't have to chase them.

"Any eggs left?" George asked.

Josie brought him the last one.

"Now what do we do?" he asked when he'd finished it.

"I'm going exploring," said Harry. "You and Jgn stay here."

"I'm coming with you!" said Josie.

So they started exploring together, leaving George to rest.

It soon turned out that the pile they were on was fresh-dug earth, and it was enclosed by some kind of holder, sort of like the thing they'd traveled in, only not really.

"This isn't part of a tree," said Josie knowledgeably. "It's what I call cold-hard. The Hoo-Mins do-diddle a lot with this stuff. I tried biting it once. Nearly broke my poison-claw. You can't burrow through it either. And sometimes," she went on, "it do-diddles all by itself."

"You mean, it's alive?"

"Oh, no," said Josie. "It's not alive."

"So how can it move and—do-diddle?" He really liked this word (and so do I).

"Don't ask me," she said. "I only know it sometimes can. When Hoo-Mins are near it. It makes big vibrations and then some brown-choke comes out of it. It smells horrible. If it comes toward you, you have to run away like mad."

"This one's completely stopped. Something very big must have bitten it."

Josie laughed her centipedish laugh, shaking up and down. "You are funny," she said. "I told you, it's not alive and it never was."

They ran and explored all over the cold-hard thing, which certainly was very big indeed. In fact it was a mechanical digger with a big heap of fresh earth in its shovel, but they didn't know that.

"Will it start to do-diddle in the bright-time?" Harry asked intelligently when they'd explored all over it.

"Yes, I expect so," she said.

"Will it move along?"

"That's what they do."

"Might it take us home?"

Josie ran round to face him. She rubbed her head against his.

"Hx," she said kindly. "It can't take us home. We're too far away, and there was all that no-end puddle in between. I don't think we'll ever get home," she finished quite cheerfully.

These were terrible, terrible words for Harry. He drooped and trailed his feelers in sadness.

"Do you mind all that much?" Josie asked.

"Yes. Because my mother's there. She's old and she needs me to look after her."

"I don't know about that. I don't think I ever had a mother that I can remember," said Josie.

"I know it's not very centipede to stay at home with your mother," admitted Harry. "I warm-heart mine. That's why I stay."

"Warm-heart? Whatever's that?"

"You don't know about warm-heart?" asked Harry in great surprise.

"Never heard of it," Josie said happily.

Harry was completely flummoxed. He had no idea how to explain love to someone who hadn't ever felt it. But he tried.

"It's a—a feeling. It makes you want to be with another, and, and—look after them."

"Doesn't sound very centipede to me," she said.

"Well, I'm as centipede as the next centipede and I warm-heart my mother, and I warm-heart Grndd, too, in a different way, and—I think it's bad manners to say something's not centipede just because you've never felt it!" he said, quite hotly for him.

"Sorry! But you two feelered me as if *I* wasn't fully centipede when you found out I was a no-meat-feeder," she said, which was so true that Harry couldn't say any more. He just rubbed her head, which was his way of saying, "I'm sorry too; let's make up."

They got back to George just as dawn was breaking, or, as a centipede would say, "Big-yellow-ball was coming back." George had managed to dig himself under the soil a bit and they only found him by smell.

"What did you find out?" he said, pushing his head out.

"We're on a cold-hard thing that moves," reported Harry importantly. "I think what we should do is go to sleep and then wake up quickly if it starts do-diddling. Maybe it'll take us somewhere where we can dig a proper tunnel and make ourselves more at home."

"Well, I hope it takes us somewhere where it isn't so cold," said George, who hadn't been running around all night. If he'd been a Hoo-Min, his teeth would have been chattering.

They didn't get much sleep. The cold-hard thing—the digger—started juddering and spluttering and coughing out brown-choke quite early in the morning. Before the centeens could wake up properly, something very upsetting happened—*upsetting* in both senses of the word. The earth they were in suddenly turned itself upside down and they found themselves falling through space.

Even when they stopped falling, the earth around them didn't. It rained down on them like the Great Dropping Damp, only instead of getting wet, they got buried.

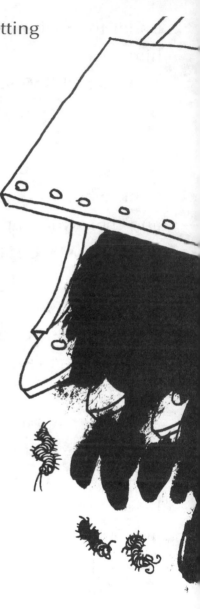

Down came
more and
more earth
until they
could feel the
weight of it on
their cuticles—so
heavy that they all
thought that if
much more fell on
them, they'd be
squashed without any
Hoo-Mins having to
stamp on them. It was
lucky their cuticles were
strong.

When the rumbling and thump-
ing of the falling soil finally stopped,
they tried to lift themselves onto their
forty-two legs, but they couldn't.

Centipedes are used to living under

the ground, but in *tunnels*, not with loads of loose soil heaped on top of them.

They couldn't even crackle to each other. Their mouth-parts were too blocked by loose grains of earth.

But they all knew what they had to do. They had to *dig*. And they did. Little by little, using their poison-claws to hollow out a space in front of them, and their legs to push away the earth, they managed to burrow their way upward. And after a long struggle, first Harry's head popped out, then Josie's. They got rid of the earth in their mouths and looked at each other.

"Where's Grndd?" they both crackled at once.

7. Josie's Big Mistake

"How can we find him?" asked Josie.

"Easy," said Harry. "Just listen."

So they listened, and then they could easily hear the tiny sounds of George's struggle underground. They both began digging eagerly, and in no time they'd made a rough tunnel to where George was. Between them they helped him out, but they were relieved to see he was doing most of it himself.

"All right," he said when they'd all cleaned their cuticles up a bit by stroking their legs over them. "Now what?"

It was bad out there in the bright-time. They couldn't make out anything with their dark-time eyes. But they could listen and smell and sense. They could hear the cold-hard thing noisily do-diddling away somewhere near them.

"That do-diddler is moving the earth," said Josie. "It's dropping it where we are. If we stay here, we'll be buried again. Let's go. Can you run, Grndd?"

George wriggled the three pairs of hurt legs. They worked pretty well. "It hurts," he said, "but I can bear it."

"You're so brave," murckled Josie. (A murckle, of course, is a murmur when it's crackled.)

Harry agreed that George was being brave, but he wished Josie hadn't said so.

"Which way shall we go?" George asked. The others lifted themselves up so that they could quest better. Harry felt baffled. The air, the smells—everything was different, unfamiliar, and alarming.

But Josie refused to be scared. "That way," she said, pointing with her feelers. "It's away from big-yellow-ball and I can sense . . . Well, I don't know what, really, but I just think we should go that way."

The others took her advice because they knew by now that Josie was very clever. But even clever centipedes, like clever Hoo-Mins, can make big mistakes.

They set off together. First they had to climb a wall of earth (the mechanical digger was dumping earth into a trench), and then they just walked and ran and walked some more across what seemed like an endless, treeless desert. They came to something they thought of as hard-ground. They felt it carefully with their feelers and front feet.

"What is it?" Harry asked Josie.

"I don't know," she said.

It seemed to make a terrifying lot of noise, anyway. They could see strange streaks of darkness rushing past, and each time one did, something like a strong wind nearly blew them away.

"I don't like this," said George. And he was right.

Where they actually were was on the edge of a busy road. Every few seconds a car or a truck or a motorbike went roaring past. Could their drivers have seen three—even quite large—centipedes scurrying across? Could they have stopped short, even if they did? Of course not.

Have you ever been driving along a main road and seen a cat or dog on the verge, obviously dying to get across, and you've wanted to shout: "Don't! Don't! You'll be run over!"

If that's how you feel about small creatures crossing busy roads, please close your eyes until I find a way to get the three friends safely to the other side.

There. You can open them. I've done it.

What do you mean, *how*? I just did. Writers can make all sorts of things happen. You don't have to know all my secrets.

You insist?

Oh . . . all right then. What happened was they had sense enough not to try to go ahead with all those black shadows racing past. So they walked *along* the road for a bit until they found a big tunnel (actually a pipe for carrying water) running *under* the road. And they went through that quite safely. The pipe was much, much bigger than their sort of tunnels, but it was dark and damp, and the centeens felt almost at home in it.

About halfway through, they had a conference. It was lucky they could signal, because the noise from overhead was so loud, they couldn't hear themselves crackle.

"Why can't we just settle down here?" suggested George, who was exhausted.

"Because for one thing, there's no earth to dig in," signaled Harry.

"And," added Josie, "for another, this place gets full of water sometimes."

They looked at her. "How do you know?"

Josie answered by running up the curve of the pipe as far as she could without falling off. "It's wet up to here. That means that's where the water comes up to." She ran down again. "And there's no food here. Not your kind and not my kind."

Still, they decided to hole-up there until dark-time. (Hole-up is a true Centiped-ish expression, by the way, that has somehow crept into Hoo-Min-speak.) They were all very tired, but it wasn't easy to sleep, as you can imagine, with all that traffic rushing and roaring over their heads. They'd never heard anything like it in their lives, and the vibrations were monstrous and fairly rattled their cuticles.

When the round ends of the tunnel were dark, they pulled themselves together and went through to the other side. A lot of the noise and vibrations had stopped, but the night wasn't quiet and pleasant like at home. At home, they'd always known when something was coming close, but here the noises arrived so quickly, and were so deafeningly loud and frightening, they got confused, or, as they would express it, upside-downed. There's nothing a centipede hates much more than being turned on its back.

"We must get away from this noise-hurt," crackled Josie. "I can't stand much more of it!"

George's injured legs were a lot better now and they were able to run fast away from the road. Soon they found themselves in a strange new place, even more difficult to understand than any of the new places so far.

There was hard-ground everywhere. And straight-up-hard-things, jutting up and up. And more noise and vibrations than ever. They scampered here and there, trying to get away from it, but only finding more. Frankly they were very lucky not to meet with a sticky end, what with all the traffic and Hoo-Mins walking about. The centeens were so upside-downed they found themselves running in circles, and if they'd been Hoo-Mins they'd have been holding their ears.

At last George signaled to the others: "Quick! Over here! I've found a tunnel!" And he disappeared through a hole in a slab of cold-hard, just big enough to admit him, and the others followed.

8. The Bad-smell Tunnels

They found themselves in a big, dark, cold, wet place. Big, dark, cold, and wet didn't bother them. But there was something that did, and that was the smell.

Centipedes have a word for it: the-smell-that-closes-your-breathing-holes. But we have a word for it too—a short one. It *stank* in there. We can hold our noses if we have to. Centipedes can't. The stench was so awful it was very hard for them to breathe.

But at least the noise-hurt had been left behind.

They soon realized that they were in another tunnel—a huge one, much bigger than the big one under the road. They ran down the rough sides of it and came to a flow of water. Well, I say water. It was water with a lot of other things in it. Not *at all* the sort of water you'd want to drink, or wash in—in fact, it was water that people had *already* drunk and washed in, if you know what I mean.

In other words—it was a sewer.

Centipedes, as you've realized, are very good at inventing new words, and before long they'd each invented their own word for this new place.

"Smell-place."

"Stink-tunnel."

"Yuck-water."

This cheered them up a bit. Then Harry said something interesting.

"It's a Hoo-Min bad-smell. Remember, Grndd, how we smelled the water that came out of the Hoo-Min nest, and it was something like this only not so disgusting?"

"How ever many Hoo-Mins would it take to make all this yuck-water?" wondered Josie.

"As many as there are soldier ants on the march," said George. And they all shuddered, because soldier ants are the worst things in the world to a centipede— even worse than Hoo-Mins. But the notion of that many Hoo-Mins all together was very scary indeed.

There was a ledge alongside the yuck-water flow and they ran along it, not really knowing where they were going, until they suddenly stopped short. Right in front of them was a creature as long as themselves, but taller, with a pointed nose, rounded ears, and brown fur. It stood there looking as startled as they felt.

It was definitely a hairy-biter of some sort. Centipedes don't really distinguish among, say, dogs and monkeys and badgers—they're all hairy-biters, dangerous threats to their lives. This one wasn't as big as those others, but they stopped just the same and got ready to run.

The hairy-biter sent a signal that was unmistakable. It showed its teeth at them— two long yellow ones under its hairy top lip and whiskers. "What are you lot doing here? This is *my* patch!"

All three centeens rose onto their back segments. Now *they* were taller. They waved their poison-claws, showing they could defend themselves. At this, the hairy-biter backed off and hastily signaled, "I'm not hunting," so they sank down again.

I think I mentioned that Harry was very good at other species' signals. He'd learned this skill while he was in a can't-get-out once with a lot of other creatures. But all those creatures you could loosely call insects. (Did you know that only creatures with three body sections and six legs are true insects? Centipedes are arthropods. Oh, you knew that? Of course you did. Sorry.)

George pushed Harry forward.

"We're not hunting," he signaled.

The creature immediately lay down, to make himself look less threatening. The centeens thought this showed very nice manners. Harry felt something polite was called for.

"We're centipedes," signaled Harry. "You?"

"I'm a rat," signaled the rat. But this was rather like two Hoo-Mins who speak different languages, saying to each other, "I'm Chinese." "I'm Swedish." Neither would be much the wiser.

Josie, Harry, and George immediately went into a huddle to pick a Centipedish name for this new acquaintance.

"Yellow-teeth?"

"Bare-tail?"

"Decent-type-hairy-biter?"

They took a very quick vote and decided on Bare-tail, which was George's, because it was the shortest. Harry went up to Bare-tail, who was still lying there quite patiently waiting, wiggling his whiskers and watching them with his beady little eyes.

"Help," Harry signaled simply.

Bare-tail stood up.

"Hungry?" he signaled, snapping his teeth and sticking his tongue out.

Harry tied several half-knots in himself, which was Centipedish for "Very hungry," but Bare-tail didn't get it. So Harry just groveled a bit in a "Yes, please" sort of way.

"Follow me," signaled Bare-tail, and, turning, scuttled off along the ledge beside the yuck-water.

9. George's Even Bigger Mistake

The whisk of Bare-tail's bare tail led them on through the darkness for some distance until they came to a sort of crack in the wall. From this was coming what we might call a mouthwatering smell, so strong that it almost drowned out the yuck-water stink.

Bare-tail poked his long nose into the crack, which was like a little cave. Another long, whiskery nose came out to meet it. They gave each other a bare-tail kiss and exchanged some signals the others couldn't understand. They guessed Bare-tail was explaining to his mate who they were, or, rather, what.

"I wonder what name he's got for us," Harry murckled.

Bare-tail turned back to them. "Eat," he signaled. He did this by taking a bite off some horrible thing in front of them and then pushing it toward them. They backed away hastily.

"Thanks, but no thanks," said Harry.

"What do you eat?" signaled Bare-tail.

George said, "Smells as if there's something really tasty in there," indicating the little cave where Bare-tail's mate was. He poked his head in. Mrs. Bare-tail, if I can put it like that, moved aside to let George look, and Harry, feeling curious, wriggled under George and stuck his head in too.

Lying in a rough sort of nest (please

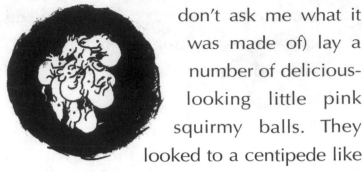 don't ask me what it was made of) lay a number of delicious-looking little pink squirmy balls. They looked to a centipede like so many cream doughnuts would to you.

"Those look good!" said George appreciatively. "Could we have one each, do you think?" And he made a move to help himself to the nearest one.

The next moment he nearly lost his head.

Mrs. Bare-tail simply flew at him and tried to bite it off. Luckily Harry, who was underneath,  reared up; she missed, George fell off backward and then Harry turned and fled like lightning—even so, feeling rodent teeth closing on three of his

back legs, he had to cast them off. Isn't it amazing that they can do that? And the legs then did their thing! Centipedes' cast-off legs have a wonderful way of wiggling even after they've come off, which distracted Mrs. Bare-tail just long enough.

"Run for it!" shouckled Harry. (A shouckle? Come now. A cross between a crackle and a shout, of course.)

It was a terrifying chase. The two bare-tails pursued the three centeens along the slimy ledge for a long way. Harry only had thirty-nine feet now that he'd cast off three, so he wasn't running his best, and he couldn't keep up with George and Josie. But then George, who was in the lead as usual, skidded and, suddenly, disappeared.

The others couldn't stop; the bare-tails were too close behind—they ran on frantically until the awful clicking sound of their pursuers' claws on the hard ledge stopped. They'd given up the chase and gone back to their nest.

Centipedes can run fast even with a few legs missing, but not for long. They run out of oxygen. Of course, the centeens didn't know that, but they knew when they were exhausted. Harry and Josie sprawled on the ledge. After a short time, a bedraggled, wet, and stinking George crawled up to them.

"What happened to you?" asked Harry.

"Fell in, didn't I," mutterckled George.

"Into the—?"

"Yes. Don't ask . . . It nearly finished me off from sheer disgust. But I remembered I knew how to swim and managed to stay afloat and keep my breathing holes out of the wet. I let the flow carry me along until I found a place where I could clamber out."

"Welcome back," said Josie.

"Now," said George after shaking himself, "will somebody please explain why those nice, friendly bare-tails suddenly turned on us like that? I thought they liked us."

"Until you suggested eating their babies," said Josie. "You fat-claw! How could you be so silly?"

"You mean those tasty little morsels were . . . Oh. Oh. Why didn't somebody tell me?"

"You've just got no centi-sense," Josie scokled.

"Well, at least I was polite about them," said George. "I said how good they looked. The bare-tails ought to have been pleased."

"I don't think so!" said Josie. "If anybody tried to eat my babies—"

"Have you got any?" asked Harry, very startled.

"Of course not. But if I did."

They stopped crackling for a bit. In fact, they all dropped off to sleep for a long time, they were so tired. When they woke up, George said, "Now what?"

"Well, we've got to get out of this breathing-hole-blocking place," said Harry. "There was a way in. There must be a way out."

"Maybe there's an Up-Pipe," said George slowly.

"What's that?" asked Josie.

"It's a dangerous tunnel that leads up to a Place of Hoo-Mins," explained Harry. "But it can't be much worse than this. Let's find one."

10. Up Another Up-Pipe

They walked the ledge slowly, looking around them, and especially upward.

Once they thought they saw quite a large tunnel up near the roof. They were just going to climb up to it when a great gush of water, looking like a rather mucky Niagara Falls to them, came pouring out and they had to run quickly forward to avoid being caught in it and washed into the yuck-river. Perhaps you can guess what *that* was.

They were beginning to think they'd

never find a suitable Up-Pipe when they saw something very interesting.

"Stop! Keep still!" whisperckled Harry, who saw them first. The other two lay flat as Harry pointed with his feelers at the wall. A double line of flat, brown, shiny creatures was crawling up and down.

"Oh! I know those," said Josie.

"So do I," crackled Harry very quietly. "Remember, Grndd? The Not-So-Big Hoo-Min fed them to us when we were in the hard-air can't-get-out."

"I never really fancied them then," he answered. "But I could eat a nest full of them now, I'm so hungry."

"They like living with Hoo-Mins and eating their food," said Josie.

Once again the others were impressed with how much she knew.

"So that means there must be a Place of Hoo-Mins up there," said Harry.

They turned their heads upward. They couldn't see much. But the brown beetle-things must have been going somewhere.

"Right. We'll go up there." George stood up. "But before we do, let's grab a snack," he said, and he and Harry shot toward one of the brown shiny things, which were actually cockroaches.

The next few seconds gave a cruel blow to the two centeens' pride. They really considered themselves about the fastest things around—it never occurred to them that they wouldn't be able to catch these beetle-things that were just ambling along. But one minute the wall and the ledge were swarming with fat crunchy-looking meals-on-legs, and the next they had vanished.

The centeens stood, baffled and empty-poison-clawed.

"Hey! Where did they go?" asked George.

"I'm sorry, I didn't get a chance to tell you," said Josie, who hadn't moved. "They're very fast. When they sense danger they're just gone. I don't think any centipede could manage to catch one. I call them faster-than-us's."

"Faster-than-us's?" said George, outraged. "How can you invent a rude name like that? Faster-than-us's? It's an insult to all centipedes!"

"Well, sorry and all that," said Josie. "But if you think you're so much quicker, why aren't you munching on one right this minute?"

"Let's not hang around here," said Harry hastily. "Let's try to get up there and see if there's a way out."

Getting up the wall was easier for a cockroach than for a centipede because centipedes are heavier. In the end, though, they did it, and there they found, sure enough, a pipe sloping upward with some cool air coming through it— air that smelled quite clean and fresh for a change.

"I hope we don't find ourselves in that awful no-top-place again," said George. He meant the city street that had been so full of noise and danger for them.

"Oh, no," said Josie. "We won't. If we were coming out there, we'd feel the vibrations already."

They crawled up the Up-Pipe. It was very smooth and hard to get a grip on, but the slope was not very steep. Little did they know how lucky they were that another gush of water didn't come rushing down to meet them and wash them back into the yuck-river, because what they were doing was crawling up the drainpipe of a Hoo-Min's kitchen sink. Luckily it was nighttime, and the

Hoo-Mins who owned the sink and the kitchen were asleep.

The three centeens emerged one by one. There was some cold-hard in the way, just at the outlet of the pipe, but they managed to squeeze past it. George, who was the biggest, got stuck, but the other two took hold of him from above and pulled him out with something like a pop.

"We can't go back that way," said George. "Not after we've had something to eat."

"We'll find another way out," said Harry comfortingly.

"We must do that right now, before we look for food," said Josie in her capable way. "We must know how to escape in case a Hoo-Min comes."

They crawled out of the sink and down to the floor of the kitchen. It was a whole lot nicer than the muck-tunnel—there were no bad smells—but it wasn't particularly clean. If you live where there are creepy-crawly things, and I include mice and ants as well as cockroaches, you mustn't leave bits of food lying about or you'll get all kinds of visitors. Of course, Hoo-Mins living in this city, far from the tropics, had no reason to expect to be visited by three large poisonous centipedes.

"We have to find a straight-up-hard-thing that moves," said Josie. "It's the way Hoo-Mins get in and out."

The other two looked at each other.

"How come you know so much about Hoo-Mins?" asked Harry.

"Well, if you must know," said Josie rather defiantly, "I once lived with them."

The other two stopped dead. "YOU WHAT!" they crackled both at once.

"Yes," she said. "I came out of my egg in a tunnel right underneath a Hoo-Min nest and that's how I grew up as a no-meat-feeder. I used to go up what you call their Up-Pipes and eat their food. I hated the meat they had. They do something to it. They make it hot somehow, and after that it's horrid, but they had plenty of other nice things. I never really learned to hunt and stop things because it was so easy to just eat tree-droppings and other things the Hoo-Mins ate."

George and Harry were flabbergasted. A centipede who lived with Hoo-Mins! It was unthinkable. *Totally* uncentipede.

"Didn't they ever hunt you?"

"No. I was careful. I only foraged in the dark-time. They never saw me. Not once."

George, struck crackle-less for a long moment, at last said, "Well. If you know so much about Hoo-Min nests, how can we get out of this one?"

"I'll show you."

She ran across the kitchen floor to where there was a door. It was slightly open. "We go through here first," she said. "After that, we just keep feeling where the fresh air is coming from and head for that."

"What if there's a straight-up-hard-thing in the way?"

"Listen, Hoo-Mins have to get in and out of their nests, just like us," she said. "There's never a place without a way out. And in an emergency, you can always hide. Their nests are full of good hiding places. Find something close to the ground and dive under that, like we did before. Now let's eat. There's lots of good food—I can smell it."

Centipedes normally like to catch live prey. They don't like eating dead things. But there wasn't much choice here. They found, and stopped, a few unwary ants (which they crunched up like peanuts), and there was a cockroach that had already stopped. When George tried eating it, he wasn't so sorry that they were faster-than-us because it was fairly disgusting. Besides, the taste reminded him of bad times.

But Josie was very happy. She found an apple core, quite fresh, under the sink, which had been  thrown at the wastebasket and missed, and lots of crumbs and some smears of jam that she got quite excited about.

"It's like tree-droppings, only much nicer!"

she said. "Do try it!" But the centeens wouldn't. They'd found a sort of dried-out puddle with some meat scraps in it.

"I wouldn't mess with that," said Josie uneasily as the other two crawled over the rim and started devouring the meat.

"Why not?" asked Harry, raising his head. George went on eating.

"I—I just don't think you should," said Josie. "There's something about that thing you're in. I don't like the smell of it."

"Smells of good meat!" said George with his mouth full.

"It smells of something alive, not stopped meat," murckled Josie. But the others were eating too greedily to listen to her. So she just stood well back, looking unhappy.

Then they found another puddle with some tasty white stuff like water in it and they hung over the rim and had a good

drink. Josie reluctantly joined in. She was too thirsty not to. But the minute she'd drunk her fill, she scuttled away from the two puddles and moved toward the door.

"I think we should go now," she said.

But as she approached the door, it began to move.

It was being pushed wider. Around the edge of it came a big, round, hairy head. The head took one look and sniffed.

Josie reared up in horror. "Look out!" she crackled.

The next moment, total chaos broke out.

11. The Hairy-yowler

Imagine a face. Straight ahead of you, but higher. It's looking down at you. It's round and furry, with pointed ears, a triangular nose, and whiskers. But the main thing about it is that it's enormous. Its face is as wide as you are with your arms stretched out, and then as wide as that again.

Now imagine that this monster is glaring at you with green eyes as big as your head, and that it then opens its mouth, which is full of teeth, makes a furious hissing noise, and takes a lunge at you.

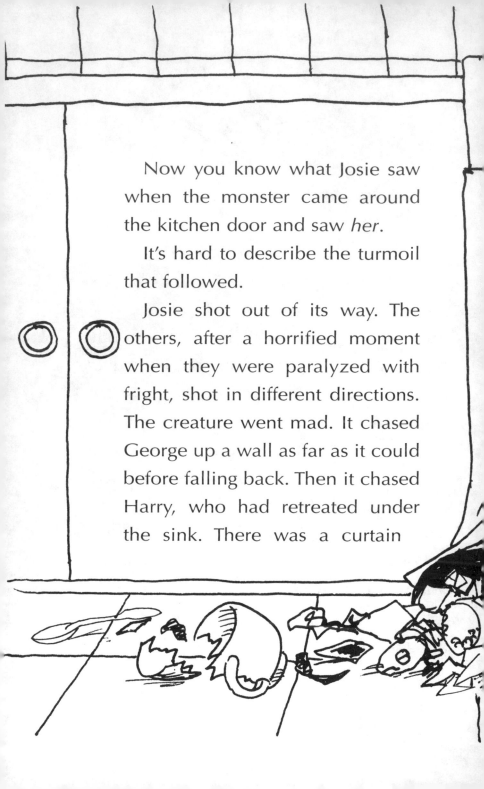

Now you know what Josie saw
when the monster came around
the kitchen door and saw *her*.

It's hard to describe the turmoil
that followed.

Josie shot out of its way. The
others, after a horrified moment
when they were paralyzed with
fright, shot in different directions.
The creature went mad. It chased
George up a wall as far as it could
before falling back. Then it chased
Harry, who had retreated under
the sink. There was a curtain

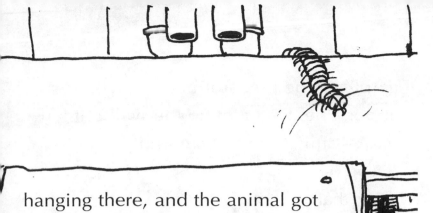

hanging there, and the animal got tangled up in it. In its struggles, it knocked over the wastebasket, which fell with a crash, scattering garbage, some of it on Josie, who was trying to get to the door.

It lost sight of Harry for the moment and saw George sliding back down the wall. It leaped toward him. Then it saw a movement and turned. Josie was crawling out from under the

garbage. The predator made a wild rush at her. She, too, shot up the wall but fell back—straight into its mouth.

You'd think that was just what it wanted, but it happened so unexpectedly that it got a fright. It jerked its head, spitting her out, and swiped her with its paw, lifting her off the ground. She clung to the paw and got in one good bite to its hairless pad before dropping off.

The cat—well, you've obviously guessed that by now—let out a sort of cat-shriek and threw itself backward, then started frantically looking for a way to escape. It seemed to have lost its sense of direction completely and kept bouncing off walls. At last, almost by accident, it found the door and fled, yowling.

The centeens flung themselves together and collapsed in a heap of feelers and legs (and heads and bodies).

"What *was* that?" gasped George.

"It was a hairy-yowler," said Josie, who, despite her close encounter, was calmer than the others. "They make a terrible noise. They chase you, but they don't like it when they catch you. I know because the Hoo-Min nest where I lived had one. I should have remembered those puddle-things where the hairy-yowlers keep their food and drink."

"You've been chased before by a hairy-yowler?"

"Oh, yes. You see, Hoo-Mins sleep in the dark-time, but hairy-yowlers don't. That's when they go hunting. So I had to be extra careful when I went foraging in the Hoo-Min nest. At first. But after one bite—mine to it, I mean; it never bit me—it left me alone. In fact, it was terrified of me."

"So when you saw this one, I suppose you weren't very scared?" asked Harry.

"Of course I was! This one didn't know me."

"It seemed to go completely crazy when it saw us."

"Oh, they do. If you're in their space, they do."

There was a pause while they caught their breath. (As we would say. Actually they were renewing their oxygen.) Then George stood up.

"Let's get out of here," he said.

They crept cautiously around the half-open door and across a big open space. "Ugh! What's this? Are we walking on a stopped hairy-biter?" asked George, picking up his feet.

In the tropics people don't often cover their floors with carpets, so this was one thing about Hoo-Mins that Josie didn't know. It made running quite difficult and slowed them down, but after a while they made it to the door on the other side of the room.

It was closed. And the carpet filled up the crack under it.

"We're can't-get-outed! We're Dried-Out!" said George. (This centipedish expression, may I remind you, is slang for "done for.")

"No, we're not!"

Josie turned and ran up something soft

117

and bunchy (it was an armchair) and from the top of it she could get onto a ledge. She ran along it till she came to an opening.

"Come on! I've found a way to the no-top-world!" she signaled to the others.

They followed her, and one by one they crept through a small space where the window hadn't been properly closed and ran down a rough wall with easy footholds to the welcoming ground below.

It felt wonderful to be free and to have earth underfoot and the no-top-world above them. True, the earth smelled different from at home—everything smelled different—and the air in their breathing-holes was very cold. But soon they would be underground in a safe, warm tunnel. Kindly darkness covered them as they ran away from the Hoo-Min nest, looking for a safe place to dig.

12. A Hard Dark-time's Work

They were in a garden. But they didn't know that.

All they knew was that there was lots of earth here: nice, loose, easy-to-tunnel-in earth. They settled on a place and began to burrow.

They burrowed all night, taking it in turns. The two at the top of the tunnel cleared away the soil as it came back. When the centeen who was digging got tired, one of the others would go down and continue the work.

None of them had ever dug a tunnel from scratch before. They'd always used tunnels dug by others, so it was a real challenge.

At first, George didn't want Josie to dig. "I'll do your share," he said gallantly.

Harry stood by, mouthparts agape. "Why?" he said.

"Why what?" asked George snappishly.

"Why will you do her share?"

"Because—well—because she's a centeena."

"So what? Can't centeenas dig?"

"Of course they can!" said Josie. If centipedes could blush, she'd have been blushing. "I don't need anyone to dig for me. Thank you just the same."

So they dug turn and turn about, and it was soon clear that Josie could indeed dig—and keep on digging longer than either of the others.

"Of course, she's younger than us," George whisperckled as the soil came spraying back up the tunnel from Josie's energetic digging.

Harry didn't say anything. He thought it was silly to offer to do Josie's share just because she was female but at the same time wondered if *he* should have offered. George seemed to know a lot more about females than Harry did. Which was strange, because George had never had a mother of his own to guide him.

And thinking of that reminded Harry of Belinda.

He'd thought a lot about her when their journey first began. But he hadn't had time since they arrived in this strange place. Now, as they worked through the dark-time, he thought of the cosy, safe home Belinda had made for him—and for George, when he visited them. He thought of how much Belinda warm-hearted him. How she'd risked her life for him several times. How she worried about him...

What must she be going through now, as dark-time followed dark-time and he didn't come back?

And who would look after her when she got too old to hunt?

What if she got so old she *stopped*, with no one beside her? It didn't bear thinking about!

"Do you think we can ever get home, Grndd?" Harry asked in a very subdued crackle.

"I doubt it, Hx," said George. "I don't see how we can."

"Oh, cheer up!" said Josie, her head coming clear as she backed out of the new tunnel. "We'll be fine right here. Nothing wrong with this! There are lots of little snacks in the earth here for you meat-feeding lot, and as for me, I can smell plenty of good tree-droppings. We'll be fine," she said again in her upbeat way. "Go on, Grndd, your turn to dig."

By the time big-yellow-ball came back, they were safe and damp in their new nest-tunnel. Josie had even crept up to the no-top-world one last time, to bring them each a leaf to sleep under.

"When we've had a good sleep, we must go on digging," Harry said. "We must have an other-way-out tunnel, in case anything comes down to get us."

"Belly-crawlers," said George gloomily. "There are bound to be belly-crawlers. Smaller than at home, like the ants are

124

smaller. Easy for them to get down our tunnel. If they do, we're Dried-Out for sure!"

Harry felt worried. He wasn't used to George being a scaredy-feelers, thinking they were Dried-Out every time there was some little problem.

"Listen, Grndd," Harry said. "Don't make out you're such a poor thing just because you got a bit of a bump. Look at me—I've had to cast off three legs and I won't get them back till the next time I shed my cuticle."

"Who said I was a poor thing?" said George. "Not me!"

"So what's the matter with you?"

"Nothing. I'm fine."

After a moment, he couldn't help adding, "Of course, shedding a few legs doesn't hurt the way something hitting you does."

The three of them curled up together under their leaves. Harry's last thoughts were about Belinda, and home.

13. A Warm Hard-air Place

Next dark-time when they awoke, Harry's first thought was food.

"Come on," he said to the others. "Let's hunt."

"I'm not hungry," said George. "I'll stay here. Maybe dig a little on the other-way-out tunnel."

Harry was amazed. George—not hungry? Unheard of!

"Shall I bring you something?" he said. "A few ants—a beetle?"

"No thanks. I couldn't face anything."

Josie and Harry set off together, back up the tunnel they'd dug the night before. "What's the matter with Grndd, do you think?" asked Harry uneasily.

"He's nest-sick."

"Grndd? I don't think so! He hasn't got a real nest of his own. He just borrows mine when he feels hungry or lonely."

Josie didn't crackle for a bit. They reached the entrance to the tunnel and poked their heads out one at a time. The night was still and scented with flowers.

"It's nice here," said Josie. "If only it were a bit warmer. I don't really want to go back. But maybe Grndd does. What was that thing you told me about—warm-heart? Maybe he's missing your mother."

This was a very unexpected idea. Harry was missing his mother. But George? Harry had always thought George just sort of used her.

"You mean, maybe he warm-hearts her like I do?"

"Well, I don't know a thing about it, but something's certainly biting him inside," she said. "Maybe it's this warm-heart thing."

They were creeping carefully about the no-top-world, questing with their feelers. Harry caught a whole raft of promising meaty smells—he hardly knew where to go first. As for Josie, she suddenly turned off at an angle and raced toward a big bush. She quickly climbed one of its stems and was soon tucking into a lot of small, round red things with a sharp smell that didn't appeal to Harry at all.

But there was something up the same stem that did. Harry followed Josie and found a big fat caterpillar curled up under a leaf. When he bit it, it dropped to the ground and he ran down and found it. It was covered with bristly hairs, which was

129

a nuisance, but he managed to get through them and suck the juicy part out, getting only a couple of the hairs in his mouth-parts.

The next thing he found was a snail.

Snails are nocturnal—that's night creatures—like centipedes. This one was very busy eating some round leaves. Harry found it by following its slime trail. But stopping it was another matter. The moment it sensed him, it shrank into its shell and stuck its underside to a leaf. Harry didn't waste time trying to bite the shell.

"Jgn!" he signaled up into the bush. "Can you come and help me?"

She scurried down to him. "What do you want?"

"Could you eat through this leaf for me so I can get at this slime-crawler?"

She took a bite out of the round leaf but spat it out. "Ugh, I don't like it; it burns my mouth-parts!"

"I'll stand on the leaf to hold it down. You just tear it away from the slime-crawler."

So they did that, and Harry had a good feast. He soon found another snail and bit this one before it could disappear into its shell.

Josie had another nibble and decided she did like the hot plant after all—especially the flower, which had a sort of tail with sweetness in it. Harry looked at her and thought how sweet *she* looked with this big orange-colored flower in her mouth-parts. It occurred to Harry that it might indeed be warm-heart that was taking George's appetite away, but not for anybody's *mother.*

"I'm going to take this other slime-crawler back to Grndd," he said hastily. "He must be hungry, whatever he says."

"Oh, all right. I'll follow you later," said Josie, munching.

When he got back to the nest, he found Grndd had cheered up a bit.

"Is that meat for me?" he said at once when he saw the snail. "Good, I'm starving. I've been working. I dug

forward," he added, showing a tunnel.
"We've got an other-way-out tunnel now.
But it's funny up there. Go up and look."

Harry scurried up the new tunnel
George had made. He emerged into a
place that was much, much warmer. After
he'd eaten, George came up behind him.

"See? It's more like at home."

The air was moist and there were lots of
strong plant smells. Harry said, "This is
good. I like this. It's the first time I've been
really warm enough since we left home."
They ran about and explored. After a
while Josie joined them.

"Oh, this is great, Grndd! How did you
find this? It's as if you'd dug a tunnel to
where we came from!" She stopped. "You
didn't, did you?"

"I don't think so," said Grndd.

"No, of course not," said Josie quickly.
"Stupid of me."

"The smells are different," said Harry. "Nice, though."

Josie was questing upward.

"I don't think this is the no-top-world," she said.

"Yes, it is," said George. "I can see white-ball."

"But there's something between him and us," said Josie.

She swarmed up a thing like a tree and found herself on a shelf. She ran about, sensing with her feelers. She bumped into something she couldn't see but which was definitely there.

She ran her feelers over it. It stretched a long way.

"There's some stuff here like hard-air," she crackled to the others.

Harry came up and joined her. "That's what it is," he said. "It's hard-air. Grndd and I were shut up in some once. You can see through it and signal through it, but you can't sense through it or go through it. It's awful stuff. I hope we're not in another can't-get-out!"

"Of course not. We can always get out through our tunnel," said Josie.

Then George said something really clever.

"Maybe the hard-air's what makes this place so warm," he said. "Because it stops cold air getting in."

No doubt by now you've guessed that George's tunnel had come up into a greenhouse. The whole idea of green-houses is to keep the air warm and moist so plants will grow better. The air in them can be just about as hot as in the tropics, so no wonder the centeens were feeling at home.

"I'm not going back to our nest," announced George. "I'm going to dig a bright-time nest and stay here—I'm sick of being cold all the time. There's plenty of earth."

"Good idea," said Josie. "I'll join you."

"I'm not so sure about this—," began Harry. But the others were already digging in the soft earth in one of the wooden seed trays that were on the shelf. They couldn't dig down far because the trays were shallow. But they felt so happy and damp and warm that they refused to worry.

And Harry, though he privately thought they should go back to their other nest deep under the ground, didn't want to be left alone. So he joined them. And when white-ball left and big-yellow-ball came back, shining on the glass roof of the greenhouse and making the air inside hotter than ever, the three centeens crawled just a little way under the soil and went peacefully to sleep.

14. Can't-get-outed!

They had a rude awakening.

Harry felt it first—a disturbance in the soil near him. Then something touched his cuticle. This made him jump, but he was still only half-awake when a mini-earthquake heaved him, and the others, to the surface.

The next second they were a wriggling, writhing heap, each one trying to discover what had happened. When they'd righted themselves (Josie had been well and truly upside-downed) they all reared up, instinctively looking for something to bite. They stood tall and clicked their poison-claws menacingly and turned their heads to see what had disturbed them.

Harry saw the Hoo-Min first. It was standing right in front of him, motionless, its huge hand poised in the air over the seed tray.

"It's a Hoo-Min!" he crackled in terror. "Run!"

They ran, as usual, in different directions. But each one was seeking the same thing —the entrance to their tunnel. They ran wildly about, trying to find the tree-thing that they'd climbed to get onto the shelf.

George found it and shot down it. Josie ran right to the far glass wall. She tried to climb down that, but there were no claw-holds and she simply slid, or fell, to the ground. As for Harry, he was so frightened he lost his wits and ran hither and thither, over one seed tray after another, until something closed over him.

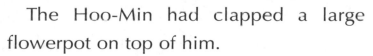

The Hoo-Min had clapped a large flowerpot on top of him.

Josie and George were running around the floor of the greenhouse looking for the entrance to their other-way-out tunnel.

But by sheer bad luck, the Hoo-Min was standing on it.

They met beside the Hoo-Min's huge foot.

"Quick! To the darkest place!" crackled George.

They fled under the lower shelf of the greenhouse into a dark corner. There was no way out. They couldn't dig—it was concrete here. They were can't-get-outed, and they knew it. It was only a matter of time before they were caught, if the Hoo-Min decided to catch them.

And he already had decided to catch them.

Now I must interrupt this thrilling story to tell you what had happened.

This Hoo-Min was the one who owned the garden and the house, complete with drainpipe, kitchen, and hairy-yowler. He also owned the greenhouse and had been working happily in it, sowing seeds in his seed trays, when he saw Harry's rear end, which was sticking up out of the earth.

A centipede's behind is rather like his front end. It has a sort of crescent-shaped bit that is his back pincer (which can also deliver a nasty, though nonpoisonous, nip), and it's attached to his last segment. The Hoo-Min immediately spotted it. Suspecting nothing more than some interesting beetle or chrysalis, he thrust *his bare fingers* into the earth to dig it out.

When the centipedes, rudely unearthed and exposed to the light, rose up against him, he got the fright of his life.

He snatched his hand away and jumped back, staring in amazement. What he saw were three enormous centipedes, at least ten times as big as any centipede he'd ever seen before. He thought he was seeing things! But when he got over his shock, he swiftly reached for a flowerpot and trapped Harry. He put a piece of brick on top. Then he took a deep breath and started hunting for the other two.

He knew enough about centipedes to guess that they would head for the darkest place. So it wasn't long before he found them.

The problem for him now was to capture them. Their problem was to avoid being captured.

It was quite a chase. They ran from one end of the greenhouse to the other along the wall under the lower shelf. The Hoo-Min was lying on the ground with his head under the shelf trying to trap them between two flowerpots, which he held facing each other like a pair of cymbals.

It was fairly easy for George and Josie

to dodge these, at first. But the Hoo-Min kept them very active and after a while their oxygen got low. First Josie lost her head and rushed into one flowerpot, which was quickly upended, trapping her underneath. Then George, sensing that she was no longer near him, doubled back on himself and ran straight into the other.

"Gotcha!"

The Hoo-Min crawled backward out

from under the shelf. He was covered with earth and cobwebs, and sweating heavily, but triumphant. He dragged the two flowerpots along the ground, holding them down firmly so the centipedes under them couldn't escape.

He clambered to his feet and stared around him. Three flowerpots. Three centipedes. He'd done it. Now what? He decided he simply had to tell someone about this amazing discovery. He left the greenhouse, closing the door carefully behind him.

...While under the pots our centeens were running desperately in circles, looking for a way of escape. Unable to crackle to each other. Scared out of their wits.

They thought their stopping-time had come.

15. Under Ground, Under Glass

Josie and George couldn't escape because their flowerpots were standing on concrete. But Harry's flowerpot was resting on a seed tray full of soft compost.

He didn't run in circles for long. He started burrowing. And while the Hoo-Min was still hurrying toward his house, Harry was free.

He shook the compost out of his breathing-holes and scuttled away as fast as he could. He found a hiding place of sorts behind a lot of close-together flowerpots (with flowers growing in them) on the shelf. It wasn't dark enough or damp enough or hidden enough, but at least he wasn't shut in anymore. He crouched there, but not for long.

It was very important to him to find out what had happened to the others.

He poked his feelers cautiously out of his hiding place. He sensed at once that the Hoo-Min had gone, so he started searching, and he soon found out where the others were. He ran down the tree-thing and sensed them through the holes in the top of their flowerpots. He swarmed over the top of George's.

"Grndd! There's a hole up here! Try to climb out!"

But George had already tried. The hole was too small.

"Try to push under!"

147

But that was no good either. The flowerpots weren't plastic; they were those heavy ones made of red clay. It seemed hopeless.

"Hx, can you see the tunnel entrance?" George asked.

"Yes. It's over there where the earth-ground is."

"Go down it to our nest. You can be safe."

"What, and leave you two? I can't do that!"

"Stupid us all getting—" George stopped because he didn't want to crackle "stopped." The thought was too awful.

"I'll tell you what," said Harry. "I'll hide in the dark place. If he tries to take you away then maybe I can be a hero, like my dad."

The Centipedish way of saying "hero" is "a centipede-that-tackles-a-Hoo-Min." Harry's father had been *stopped* after biting a Hoo-Min, so George knew at once what Harry had in mind. The thought made him shiver from one pair of pincers to the other.

Harry was planning to attack the Hoo-Min who had can't-get-outed them.

"Don't do it, Hx!" came a crackle from Josie's flowerpot. "You'll be stopped for sure!"

"Not for *sure*," said Harry bravely. "My mother tackled a Hoo-Min once and *she* didn't get stopped." He paused to think how incredibly proud his mother would be if he became a hero. Except that of course she'd never get to hear about it.

They didn't crackle any more. There was no more to crackle. Harry curled up in the dark place under the shelf and waited, and the other two waited under their flowerpot can't-get-outs. They were all very scared. Quite soon, the Hoo-Min

149

opened the door and came back into the greenhouse. And he brought another Hoo-Min with him.

Now, most Hoo-Mins, confronted with enormous tropical centipedes in their greenhouse, would simply try to kill them. Hoo-Mins are horribly inclined to kill anything they don't recognize—no matter how much bigger they are and how little they actually have to fear. Or how unusual or interesting their find may be.

But not this Hoo-Min.

This Hoo-Min happened to be very interested in small life forms. He was, in fact, what we call an entomologist—that is, someone who studies insects. So when he got over his shock at seeing the three centipedes in his greenhouse, he was actually very excited—not least because he simply couldn't imagine how they had got there.

And now he'd caught them! He wasn't sure what he was going to do with them, so he'd hurried back to his house to get some advice from one whom I will call Mrs. Hoo-Min.

She was rather special, too. Many female Hoo-Mins are scared of creepy-crawlies, but not this one. She was almost as excited as her mate about this extraordinary find. She had thought of a way to transfer the captives from their flowerpots into a box— a box with a sheet of glass on top so that they could be studied.

"Let's put the one on the seed tray into the box first, before it digs its way out," she said, swiftly summing up the situation. She lifted the flowerpot and seed tray together and quickly emptied them into the cardboard box.

Nothing came out (except compost).

"Oh no!" she said. "It's gone!"

And now she *was* scared. Because it's one thing to have a poisonous centipede trapped under a flowerpot and another thing to have it running around loose, who knows where. So she started crackling—sorry, I mean *saying*—some rather unkind things to the Hoo-Min about being careless and silly.

The Hoo-Min waited till she'd finished and then said, "Well, don't panic, because I know where it is. It's behind these pots." Which is certainly where Harry *had* been—but he wasn't there now.

The Hoo-Mins moved every pot and seed tray and bag of compost and tool in the greenhouse, but they didn't find Harry. At last the Hoo-Min—rather bravely, I must say—lay down on the ground again and started poking about with a long stick into the dark corners.

Which is where Harry said he was going to hide. But he wasn't there now. Can you guess where he was? The safest place?

Yes! Right. While the Hoo-Mins had been searching down the far end of the greenhouse, he'd decided the best place was in the tunnel leading to their underground nest, so he'd rushed into that, and he was down there feeling the vibrations of those big feet on concrete and earth. Waiting for his chance to be a hero.

16. The Middle of the Dark-time

In the end, the Hoo-Mins had to give up the search.

Mrs. Hoo-Min did a trick with the sheet of glass, slipping it under the other two flowerpots and tipping George and Josie into the cardboard box. Then she put the glass on top and the Hoo-Mins peered down at the two centipedes through this glass lid. Mrs. H was absolutely amazed by how big they were.

"How on earth did they get here?" she said. "Where could they have come from?"

"Either they escaped from some collection, or they stowed away in some shipment from a tropical country," said her mate. "You hear of creatures traveling in crates of fruit sometimes."

"Poor things! So far from home. They must be cold here."

"Oh, come on," said the Hoo-Min. "You'll be worrying about them missing their mothers next. Let's take them into the house and have a good look at them."

But this was too much for Mrs. H.

"Excuse me! They're not coming into the house!" she said. "They can stay out here."

"Oh . . . But I've got all my books and equipment in my study—"

"No."

"Well. Maybe you're right. Just look at the size of them! Look at those forcipules!"

"Those what?"

"Forcipules," the Hoo-Min repeated proudly. "That's the scientific name for their poison-pincers. I wouldn't like to get a nip from one of those!"

"Exactly," said Mrs. H firmly.

The two Hoo-Mins stayed in the greenhouse for a long time, looking at George and Josie through the sheet of glass. The Hoo-Min proudly told his mate quite a lot about this particular kind of centipede. He knew their Latin name right off by heart.

"These amazing creatures, my dear, are not just common or garden centipedes. They are scolopendromorphs. Skolo—pendro—morphs. Or, if you prefer, you can call them scolopocryptops."

"Skolo—poc—rip—tops!" repeated Mrs. H. "That makes them sound a bit like dinosaurs!"

"Dinosaurs?"

"Yes! Triceratops, those sorts of names! Oh, isn't this exciting!"

"Do you realize that centipedes have been on this planet nearly as long as dinosaurs? Much longer than us humans. I really can't wait to look them up on the Internet!"

Meanwhile, Harry was under the Hoo-Mins' feet, and George and Josie were under their faces. Harry was safe enough, and in a nice, dark, damp place, but the others had nowhere to hide from the light, so they couldn't have been more unhappy.

After what seemed like forever, the Hoo-Mins took off.

Harry promptly popped up out of the tunnel and ran up the tree-thing. He was soon slipping and sliding on the glass covering of his friends' can't-get-out.

"Why didn't you *bite them?*" was George's first signal. Which was a bit unfair of him, after nobly urging Harry to save himself.

"Because they weren't taking you away," said Harry, rather hurt. "If they try to take you away, I'll tackle them all right! Both of them!" How he was going to bite two Hoo-Mins at once he didn't stop to ask himself.

"Please don't leave us!" pleaded Josie. So Harry lay down on the glass lid to be as near his friends as possible, and they all just had to wait to see what would happen.

* * *

What happened was that in the middle of the dark-time, the door of the greenhouse quietly opened and the Hoo-Min came back in. Harry was getting ready to run, but suddenly a stream of light hit him. It was like something pinning him to the spot—he got dazzled and couldn't move.

The beam of light was of course a flashlight that the Hoo-Min had brought.

When he shone it on the box, the first thing he saw was Centipede Number Three on top of the glass.

"Sociable little fellows, aren't you?" he said as he dived for a flowerpot.

Harry ran like mad, but the beam of light followed him, blinding his eye-clusters. He turned this way and that, not so much to escape the Hoo-Min as to escape the horrible blinding light. In no time, the flowerpot came down and he was trapped again. It was almost a relief to be in darkness.

Before he knew it, he was in the box with the others.

17. Centi-heroes

The Hoo-Min picked up the box and left the greenhouse.

He carefully switched off the flashlight while crossing the garden and went into the house. There he took the box to a room that was his study and put it on a big table. He closed the door quietly. Then he switched the top light on.

Light flooded into the box and the poor centeens ran around and around trying to avoid it, but they couldn't, and in the end they just huddled together in a corner.

Where, you might ask, was Mrs. Hoo-Min at this point? The same Mrs. H who had forbidden her mate to bring centipedes into her home? Well, she was fast asleep in bed. The Hoo-Min was doing this behind her back. That was the reason he was being quiet.

Now the Hoo-Min began to study his captives seriously. He had some big books with lots of pictures of centipedes and other creatures open in front of him. He had a large magnifying glass and a notebook in which he began making notes and drawings. His computer was switched on and he had called up a website all about giant centipedes. He was having a wonderful time.

The trouble was he didn't know where to stop. He didn't think anyone would believe how big his centipedes were—unless he measured one.

Of course, he wasn't stupid enough to try to do this without taking precautions. He had a pair of very thick gardening gloves made of leather that he was pretty sure no centipede could pierce with his— ahem!—forcipules.

But there was a problem. The gloves were so very thick that they made him clumsy, so he decided to use only one of them—the one for the left hand. He would hold a centipede down (gently) with his gloved hand and measure it. He needed his right hand free to do the measuring, which was rather a delicate operation.

He lifted the glass carefully off the box.

"I'll measure the biggest," he muttered to himself. "When I write my article for a scientific journal, I want to make it as impressive as possible." And he reached his gloved hand into the box.

The centeens did exactly what the

Hoo-Min had expected. They cowered into the corner. "Small creatures run away," thought the Hoo-Min. "They don't attack unless they're cornered." He smiled to himself, because the centipedes *were* cornered. He was sure they would be too scared to do anything but keep as far away from him as possible.

Now, he had to do this quickly. He made a lightning grab for George with the gloved hand. He caught him by the back of the head and pulled him out of the box.

George writhed and twisted and wriggled and writhed some more. He tried to escape. He tried to bite. He raised his back end and tried to nip with his back pincers.

He got hold of the glove and tried to pierce it, but it was too thick for him.

Meanwhile, the Hoo-Min was struggling to lay a ruler alongside George and measure him. But George was wriggling so much that he couldn't.

So the Hoo-Min got clever. Holding George's head-end with his gloved hand, he got hold of the tail-end with his ungloved hand, just above the pincers (remember, the back pincers are not poisonous), and stretched George's body quickly and carefully next to the ruler.

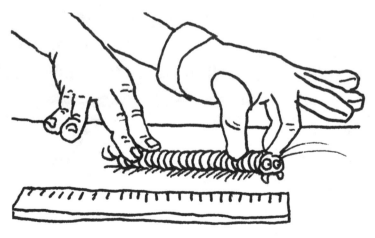

He just had time to say "seven inches!" in a tone of wonder before he let out a howl of agony.

He'd been wrong—so wrong—about centipedes not attacking.

If he'd just read a little further on the website, he'd have discovered that giant centipedes can be very aggressive. It might not have added "especially when their friends are in danger," but you and I know that it should have.

The Hoo-Min was dancing around the room, alternately shaking and gripping his right hand with its bitten finger. Twice bitten. Once by Harry, once by Josie. He was making the most extraordinary noises.

They were extraordinary because, after

the first howl, he was trying not to howl anymore, although it was hurting like mad.

He didn't want Mrs. H to hear him.

Unfortunately, she already had.

A few moments later she threw the door open and rushed in in her dressing gown, crying: "My dear, whatever's happened? What's the matter?"

She didn't even notice that as she rushed in, three very swift arthropods rushed out.

18. A Very Lucky Non-escape

Luck is one of the most important things in this life.

And luck doesn't just happen to Hoo-Mins. It happens to centipedes, too.

Now, you might think that the luckiest thing that could happen to Harry, George, and Josie at this point would be to find the front door of the house open so they could make their escape.

But just think what would have happened if they had. They'd have found themselves back in the big city, with all the traffic and hard pavements and not much to eat *and* lots of Hoo-Mins just wanting to kill (sorry, stop) them. A life of fear, probably quite short.

So it's lucky, to start with, that the front door was not open, though with Josie in the lead they made a dash for it. She knew where it was because she could feel a draft coming under it. A very thin sort of draft, because the space under the door was thin. Far too thin for them to squeeze through.

They stopped and turned. They meant to run back the way they'd come and try to find another way out. But they couldn't. Because walking slowly and menacingly along the floor toward them was their old enemy, the cat.

I'm sorry to hurt the feelings of any cat lovers among you, but cats are not the brightest of animals. You'd think this cat would take one look at his tormentors and run a mile. But it had sort of forgotten about Josie biting it. It saw these wiggly things and its instinct told it to investigate them. So instead of running away from them, it ran toward them.

They fled behind an umbrella stand in a corner of the hall.

This was a good move. The cat couldn't get at them now. It made a few cautious dabs with its paw (and nearly got it bitten again) and then decided to sit down and wait for them to come out.

There was a lot of noise coming from the study. Mrs. H was really very upset about her mate's going against her wishes. I'm afraid she wasn't awfully sympathetic about him getting bitten once she saw that he was only in agony and not about to die.

He, meanwhile, saw no reason now to hold back his howls—in fact he saw a reason to howl louder. He wanted Mrs. H to realize how painful the bites were and maybe be a bit kind to him after all.

They were both very worried about the centipedes being loose.

Before long, Mrs. H had to ring for an ambulance. The phone was in the hall, and after making the call she turned around and saw the cat staring very hard into the corner where the umbrella stand stood. She understood at once where the missing centipedes must be.

She summoned her mate.

"They're behind the umbrella stand," she said.

"Oh, oow, ohh," he moaned. "When's the ambulance coming?"

"Soon. What are we going to do?"

The Hoo-Min said something rude about not having the slightest idea.

Mrs. H lost her temper.

"You are hopeless!" she said. "Go and get those gloves."

He tottered off and got the gloves. She put them on. Then she took a jacket off a peg in the hall.

"Get ready to lift the umbrella stand away when I tell you," she ordered her mate.

"I can't lift anything. My hand—!"

"Oh, forget your hand! Pull it then. Now!"

The Hoo-Min jerked the umbrella stand away from the corner, and like lightning Mrs. H threw the jacket on top of the centeens.

The cat thought it was a game and pounced on the jacket.

Mrs. H yelled at the cat, and it fled.

She fell to her knees, quickly pushed the edges of the jacket toward the middle, and with great skill flipped it over and gathered it into a sort of bundle, with all the centeens inside. She shook them down into the bottom and held all the open edges tightly together. (Ah, you thought they might run out through the sleeves? Sorry, she held those too.)

"Now bring me a box with a lid," she said to her mate, who was standing there with his mouth open. He didn't look a bit like a clever entomologist, but then probably the poison was surging through him, stopping his brain from working. "There's one in the garage. Hurry!" The poor Hoo-Min staggered away.

By the time the ambulance arrived to take the Hoo-Min to the hospital, the centeens were once again can't-get-outed.

So where's the good luck in that? you may ask.

You'll see.

19. Some Even More Wonderful Good Luck

Mrs. H forgot to shut the cat up, but luckily cats aren't as clever even as honey badgers (you'll know what I'm talking about if you've read Harry's other adventures), or maybe they're just not as strong. Although it certainly tried, it couldn't get the lid off the box. It scratched the outside with its claws, though, giving the centeens another awful scare. Really, it was all getting to be too much—they were feeling worn out. But Josie was the calmest.

"What's going to happen to us?" George waickled. "If the hairy-yowler doesn't get us, the Hoo-Mins will!"

"What do you think, Jgn?" asked Harry.

"I think the hairy-yowler can't get in here. And I think the Hoo-Mins don't want to stop us or they would have done it by now."

"Especially when we bit one. That's when Hoo-Mins usually stop you, when you bite them," said Harry.

"All it did was yowl louder than the hairy-yowler," said Josie, and that gave them a bit of a centi-giggle.

The cat gave up and went away. And soon afterward the Hoo-Mins returned. The first thing they did was have a peep in the box.

"What do you think we should do with them?" Mrs. H asked.

The Hoo-Min was feeling a bit better

now after whatever they'd done in the hospital. Certainly his brain must have been working.

"I've decided we should take them to the zoo," he said.

"That's a good idea," said his mate with relief. She'd been afraid he might want to keep them.

This is where the real good luck begins to kick in. Because if there's one thing that zoos do not do to creatures, however creepy-crawly or poisonous, it's stamp on them. So at least the centeens were not going to be stopped.

Not that they knew that. And even if they had had the slightest idea about zoos, they would have expected to be kept in some can't-get-out for the rest of their lives.

The Hoo-Mins took the box, which now had holes punched in the lid and a lot of string around it, to the zoo.

It was a big zoo because it was in a big city. It was quite famous for its Insect House, which was for arthropods and arachnids (that's spiders to you) and other sorts of creepy creatures as well.

The Hoo-Mins had telephoned in advance, so there was a lot of excitement at the zoo. They were shown into a room in the middle of the Insect House and invited to display their prize to several experts.

As soon as the lid came off the box, there was a buzz of interest. Several huge Hoo-Min faces bent over the box for a closer look. The centeens got panicky

and ran about, and Harry raised himself threateningly, but he couldn't reach what he would have liked to bite— one of the big noses poking down at him from above.

"But—good heavens! Is it possible? Aren't these—"

"They can't be! So far from—"

"They are, though, I'll swear it! They're—"

Then there was a great rummaging among books, a poising of magnifying glasses, a putting of heads together, and a lot more Hoo-Min mouth-noises.

Our Hoo-Min—the entomologist—was soon being banged on the back and congratulated on a truly awesome find.

"What you have found," he was excitedly told, "are three remarkable specimens of *scolopendra gigantae rara extremis marvellosa*! One of the rarest of the giant centipedes! They were thought till recently to be extinct. We have a program for trying to reestablish them in their native habitat. Just as soon as we can arrange it, we must fly them back to where they came from."

"Do you know where that is?"

"Oh yes, of course we do. They come from a very limited area of—well, we can't tell you exactly where, because it's secret. You know there are collectors who would give anything to get a hold of one of these little beauties. Centipedes, believe it or not, are becoming very popular as collectors' items. They change hands for a great deal of money."

"Do you mean they're valuable?"

"Very valuable. But of course, as a scientist you wouldn't be interested in that side of things. What satisfaction you'll get from restoring these rare and wonderful creatures to the wild and helping to save them from extinction!"

"Ah . . . yes, of course," said the Hoo-Min, putting his bitten finger into his mouth and sucking it thoughtfully. He dared not look at Mrs. H, who might not be quite sure that science was the main thing and that it didn't matter a bit that they weren't going to get any money.

The three centeens were put into a glass-fronted case that the zoo people had carefully lined with leaf litter, rotting wood, soil to dig in, and bits of branches to crawl up. And they were supplied with the right kind of food.

Well. Not really. Even the best zoos can't provide the mixed diet of living things that centipedes and other meat-eaters really like to hunt. They certainly didn't know enough to give Josie any fruit. I have no doubt that our three heroes would have been deeply unhappy in the zoo, and Josie might have starved if they'd had to stay there long.

But their centipedish luck was with them. They only had to stay in the zoo for a very short time.

They'd been in the newspapers, but they didn't know that. What they soon noticed, though, was that many Hoo-Mins came to visit them.

They got quite used to the enormous faces peering in at them through the hard-air. I'm afraid George got to be a bit of a show-off, once he'd realized the Hoo-Mins couldn't get at him. He would run up and down the tree branch, pose on his rear segments, click his poison-claws ("Oooh, Mommy, look, he wants to bite us!"), and twist himself into hunger-knots.

"Oh, do stop it, Grndd, you look so silly!" Harry kept saying. But George crackled, "If we have to live in this boring can't-get-out, at least let's have a bit of fun teasing the Hoo-Mins!"

Josie crackled nothing. She was *really* hungry, so hungry that she seriously thought of trying to stop being a no-meat-feeder, but when she tried an earwig and then later a woodlouse, they tasted so disgusting she found she simply couldn't. So she spent most of her time lying under some leaf litter saving her energy.

The others were very worried about her. They were worried about themselves as well. They had no idea if they were ever going to get out, and as for getting home—even Harry had despaired of that.

But one happy, lucky day they were lifted out of the case on the end of a long stick-thing, packed away in a special box, and taken to an airplane, which flew them all the long way back to the hot tropical country they had come from. No, I can't tell you which it was, either, because I don't want collectors coming along looking for them. Some of these people don't care *what* becomes extinct so long as they have a specimen of it.

When the centeens got there, there was a little ceremony among the Hoo-Mins because they were so pleased to have three of this rare kind of centipede to return to the wild. And then the centeens were released.

Harry and George knew at once that they were not far from their dear home-tunnel. They were two very excited and happy centeens.

Only one thought threatened to spoil the great happiness Harry felt. Can you guess what it was?

Yes, of course. They'd been away for such a long time. He was very much afraid that Belinda wouldn't be there to welcome them home.

20. Blocked!

They couldn't find the home-tunnel at
first. It seemed to have lost its special
smell somehow, and that disturbed both
Harry and George a lot, though neither of
them said anything to the other. It should
have smelled strongly of home, and of
Belinda, but it didn't. They only found it
because of other smells nearby that
hadn't changed.

"Here it is! Here it is!" crackled Harry
at last, and dived down the entrance with
George just behind him. Josie stayed in

the no-top-world and waited. It's very bad centi-manners to enter another centipede's home unless you're asked.

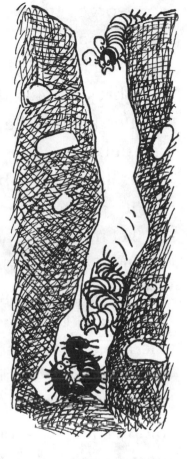

Harry was rushing down the tunnel so fast that he wasn't feelering where he was going. He actually crashed into something headfirst, and all his segments kind of squashed into each other like a concertina.

George then ran into the back of Harry and they got all tangled up.

"It's blocked!" crackled Harry. "Some earth's fallen down! Mama—"

George twisted himself straight. Without a crackle he got in front of Harry and began to dig.

"That's why it didn't smell right," he mutterckled. "The home-smell couldn't get out."

"Is the fall very bad?"

"It's not new. The earth's packed tight."

"Let me dig!" crackled Harry frantically. He tried to crawl on top of George to dig where he was digging, but there was no room. He backed off and stood behind George. If centipedes could dance with impatience, he would have danced.

"Why didn't she dig herself out? Why didn't she—" He broke off as he remembered something. "Grndd! Stop. There's an other-way-out tunnel! Let's try that."

The two centeens had to back out—there was no room to turn. As their back ends, and then the rest of them, emerged one after the other, they found Josie waiting for them.

"Is the one you warm-heart all right?" she asked at once.

Harry couldn't crackle. George said, "There's been an earth-fall. We have to find another way into the nest. While we do, would you mind going down there and digging? In case the other way is blocked too."

"Yes, I can do that," said Josie. She could sense that Harry was in a bad way, and she rubbed his head with hers in crackle-less sympathy, even though she'd said she didn't know about warm-heart. Actually, if anyone had asked her, she might not have been so sure of it now. "Don't worry, you'll find her," she whisperckled.

Then she ran down the tunnel. The other two started questing about on the no-top-world. They'd both used the other-way-out tunnel a few times, mostly when they were playing, but not for ages, and they weren't at all sure where it came out. They were trying to find Belinda's scent. They couldn't. They hunted for it for a long, long time. Harry was beginning to feel quite desperate when they sensed Josie's signal.

"Over here!"

They both rushed over to her. Her head was sticking out of a hole under a lot of dead leaves and rotting stuff.

"I got through the earth-fall, and then I

just ran through your nest and found this other-way-out tunnel. It isn't blocked; you can go right down."

Harry stood still. He dared not ask.

"Was—was there any—centipede—down there? In the nest?" It was George who found his crackle first.

"Well—no—only a stopped one."

There was a terrible crackle-lessness.

George recovered first.

"Wait here, Hx."

He ran down the other-way-out tunnel. Josie stayed with Harry.

Harry was lying flat on the ground. His feelers were drooping as far as they could go. His whole body felt limp with misery. His mama must have stopped. Down

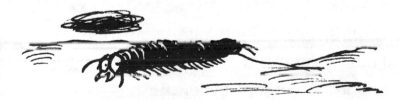

there in their empty nest all alone. It was too awful. It was *too awful.*

George shot out of the hole.

"It's not her, Hx!"

Harry stood up. "Not her?"

"There's an empty cuticle down there. But it's not her. It's not long enough to be her. Some other one of us must have gone down there and stopped. She's not there." Harry was stiff with hope. He waved his feelers in all directions.

"So she must have left our nest. She probably went hunting for us. She's done that before when we didn't come home. We must find her!"

Thus the big search started.

When you're desperate for help, you'll take it from anything or anyone, and Harry's view of his fellow creatures quickly changed. When he met one, no matter how tasty, he didn't look on it as prey but as a possible helper in his search for his mother. It was like when he'd once made friends—*friends!*—with a lady dung beetle. Or when he had learned to talk to a tarantula, though that hadn't been friendly at all. Not to mention the bare-tail.

Now he used his skill at signaling to other species. Every creature, large or small, that he met he asked, as best he could, if they'd seen a big-female-one-like-him. None of them had, or else they just didn't get it. Or else they ran away fast and didn't even try to understand him.

George and Josie, who had no gift for languages, just ran around looking. Only George knew Belinda's scent, so Josie kept close to him.

Harry went his own way. He refused to

give in to tiredness or hunger. He saw a rhinoceros beetle and gave chase. It ran away from him, but he ran faster. He got in front of it.

"I'm not hunting!" he signaled. The

beetle stood still, scared and puzzled, its horn lowered just like a real rhinoceros. Harry struggled to form a signal in beetle, a language that always rhymes. It was very hard—he wasn't that good.

"You see—like me? Left behind, now can't find. If you know, you show—and I'll never hunt you!" All right, the last bit doesn't rhyme at all, but it seemed Harry got his message across. He saw a gleam of understanding in the beetle's tiny eyes. It set off at a slow amble. Harry came after it. He wasn't sure if it was leading him somewhere or just going about its business. Either way, Harry was half-stopped with impatience. He began to run around it in circles, trying to hurry it up, but it was a rather old rhinoceros beetle. It couldn't, or wouldn't, hurry.

It walked a long way. Harry could hardly bear the suspense.

At last it stopped by a hole—an entrance.

"One went there, that's its lair," it signaled.

Harry feelered the air. Yes! *Yes!* He could smell her! She was down there. His little heart soared with relief.

"Thank you, pank you, mank you!" he burbackled to the beetle. If he'd been a

Hoo-Min, he'd have kissed it right on its horn.

It looked a bit puzzled, as well it might. But it got the message.

"Done my best. You do the rest." As Harry started down the tunnel, the old beetle followed him with a last signal: "Don't forget! That we met!" This was its way of reminding Harry to keep his promise never to hunt it. (I'm happy to tell you that of course Harry did. And didn't. In fact, he never stopped another rhinoceros beetle, just in case.)

Harry raced down the tunnel. She was alive! She was here!

He forgot the others—he forgot everything. His mama was waiting for him!

He rounded a bend in the tunnel and it opened into a typical centi-nest. And there she was—Belinda—Bkvlbbchk—his mama.

She was lying under a faded, dried-out leaf. She looked terribly old and *almost* Dried-Out herself.

As he came near, his feelers swiveling with excitement and happiness, she raised her head.

"Who is it?" she crackled faintly.

"It's me, Mama. I'm back."

"Hx? My Hxzltl? My very own dear centi?" She crawled out weakly from under the leaf and circled him, touching him now and then with wondering feelers. He could see she couldn't walk very well. When she got to his rear end, she exclaimeckled: "Hx—you've lost three of your legs!"

"Don't worry about that, Mama! They'll

grow again when I next shed my cuticle."

"But how did you lose them?"

"It's a long, long story, Mama."

"Tell it to me. Oh, tell it to me!"

"Of course I will! Only I have to let the others know we're here."

"Others? Grnddjl is back, too?"

"Yes, and a centeena we met called Jgnblm. You'll like her, Mama, and she'll like you."

"Oh, please, don't go away again yet! I've missed you so much!"

He gave her a centi-kiss, stroking her old head gently with his feelers.

"Don't worry, Mama. I promise I'll never leave you again."

Epilogue

There's one thing more I have to tell you about. It's not so much to do with Harry, but I think it's interesting.

Belinda explained that she'd had to move out of the old nest because she wasn't strong enough to dig through the earth-fall and was afraid of another. But now they moved back—all of them.

Harry and George made Belinda comfortable, with a fresh, damp leaf, and started feeding her up with lots of tasty treats. Josie, who moved in with them, helped, and even persuaded Belinda to give tree-droppings a try. Belinda soon got a lot better, what with having her hunting done for her and her centeens around her. Plus her centeena, who before long was a full-grown female centipede.

One dark-time, Josie produced something like a little bundle. It was full of eggs. And soon after that, a mass of tiny wriggling soon-to-be-giant centipedes hatched out. (Josie certainly did her bit to stop *Scolopendra Gigantae Rara Extremis Marvellosa* from becoming extinct, though of course she didn't know that.)

Now, the idea of being a grandmother doesn't really come into it with centipedes. Most of them don't even care about mothers very much. But as you must know by now, Belinda and Harry had a special relationship—making them exceptional centipedes.

Belinda was surprised and delighted by the happy event.

Josie made a centi-basket for her babies and looked after them tenderly. And Belinda helped her.

She also interfered sometimes. She pushed the babies back into the basket when they tried to climb out. She hintackled to Josie that baby centis need *meat*, not just tree-droppings, and when Josie wasn't looking, Belinda sneaked them bits of chewed-up worm and spiders' legs. But Josie was very patient with her. It's good to have some company and advice when you have your first thirty babies.

And where, do I hear you ask, were Harry and George while all this was going on? Male centipedes are, I'm bound to say, absolutely useless as fathers. They were off hunting and having more adventures. Not that they ever went far away again. Harry kept his promise to Belinda about *that*.

And when all the baby centipedes were ready, they crawled out of the basket and ran away in all directions.

Nearly all.

One of Josie's babies stayed in the nest and, when he was big enough, began to give plenty of worry to his mother (who by this time knew all about warm-heart). Not to mention Belinda, his—

No. This was one thing the centipedes never invented a word for. So I'll have to do it.

How about centi-gran?

Or granny-pede, if you prefer.